About the Author

Dreena Collins lives in the island of Jersey, in the Channel Isles.

Her first short story collection was The Blue Hour: fourteen character-based tales exploring challenges, such as dementia, obsession, and loneliness. She has also been published in the *Eyelands* International Collection, Luggage, as well as having poems and articles published in several periodicals and magazines.

Dreena has been shortlisted and longlisted in several writing competitions, including the Mslexia Annual Short Story Competition.

Dreena's hobbies include eating Thai food, unintentionally waking at 4.30 a.m., and falling over.

http://dreenawriting.co.uk
facebook.com/dreenawriting
Instagram.com/dreenawriting
Twitter: @dreenac

Foreword

The stories in this collection form volume two in The Blue Hour series. They include 'The Mirror', which was placed in the top 100 of The Bridport Prize in 2016, 'Change', long-listed in the Retreat West short story competition in 2018, and 'At Night She Came Alive', shortlisted in Fish Publishing annual flash fiction competition, in 2019. You will also be reacquainted with two characters from volume one – Arthur, and his son, Edward.

As with volume one, I wrote many of these stories in the early hours, and in snatched moments throughout the week - between work, grumpiness, family time and food. Some of them came to me in a flash, and others are re-workings of older pieces, resurfacing afresh after heavy editing and modification.

With both collections, my intention has been to explore the types of challenges and moments that many of us experience in the contemporary world. I wanted to give time and space to everyday people, with ordinary themes and experiences that can seem utterly extraordinary to those experiencing them: loss, love, mental health challenges. Abuse.

And also, I do love a twist.

If you enjoy these tales, please leave a review for me. You have no idea the difference this can make.

Dreena Collins

The Day I Nearly Drowned
and other stories

Short Stories Vol. Two

Copyright © Dreena Collins 2019. All rights reserved.

First published in 2019.

ISBN: 978-1-9993735-2-8

Cover design by Dreena Collins

Back cover quote courtesy of Georgie Bull, author, freelance content writer and blogger: www.georgiebull.com.

Back cover quote two courtesy of Patrick Sheil, author of 'Kierkegaard and Levinas: The Subjunctive Mood'.

Silhouette art modified from images appearing at: www.clipartqueen.com

Contents

1. More Little Gems
2. A Screech of Gulls
3. Jessica Was Nice
4. Change
5. She Walks Through Mud
6. The Mirror
7. Petrichor
8. (Not) Prone to Winking
9. Boulder
10. The Day I Nearly Drowned
11. A Pane of Glass Between Them
12. Bedtime Story
13. Sleep on It
14. Incendiary
15. French Knitting on a Cotton Reel

More Little Gems

Arthur walked past me, carrying a cup of tea, flickering, tremoring – the mug ready to turn as a shooting star.

It was hard not to move, not to jump up, intervene. But he would not have thanked me. I resisted the urge - trusting instead to the plastic vessel, with its lid and insultation, to prevent any major injuries.

He hated that mug.

He had finally given in when a scolding hot cup had flown as a swarm into the air last month – its spray hitting a wall, a side board, a chess set. His right foot. His already flaky skin had been left bubbled and punctured for a week afterward. Then he relented. Only then.

This was the first time he had been out of bed for days. As he walked, he huffed his cheeks in a billowing motion, rhythmically puffing in and out as jellyfish, while he tried fruitlessly to disguise the effort. Walking from kitchen to sofa was enough to put him out of breath. This would be enough to send him to sleep, I guessed – after the tea, of course.

"Humph," he said, as he sat down on the sofa beside me. He did not look at me.

"OK, dad?" I asked.

"What? Yes, yes," he burst out, gruffly, "Yes."

He thought for a minute. Then nodded his head, face down, towards the plastic tea.

"Are you alright?" he asked.

"Yes, dad."

"Do you want a cup of tea?"

He turned to look at me, lips slightly parted, dry; his eyes lost, drowning in an oily film.

"I'm fine, dad."

He had already asked me twice.

I reached across for the remote from the little table he had, the same little mahogany table he had owned since before mum died. The remote was large, scratched - a little grimy.

"There'll be a movie on," I said.

A few channels later, and I settled on an animation full of primary colours, talking animals, re-workings of sixties pop songs. Dad chuckled, seemed happy enough. There was a time when he would have barked at me for choosing this – it made me slightly sad to find that he no longer did.

I leant back on the sofa and glanced over at him as he laughed to himself and shook his head, intermittently swigging from his beaker. He was a different man. He was a shadow, an impression of my dad, a reflection in a lake that shifted and buckled under ripples and wrinkles in front of my eyes. Inconstant. Delicate. Unstable.

After around thirty minutes, his head began to loll. I reached over and took the plastic mug from his lap: gently unfurled his warm, fat fingers from the handle. He had only drunk half of his tea.

I left the film on, thinking that muting the sound might disturb him. I wasn't sure if this change of scene from his bedroom to the living room had been a good idea. He seemed to have enjoyed it, but it had clearly exhausted him. I worried what the impact would be – and yet at the same time, there was only one end in sight. What difference could it really make? If he was happy, and comfortable.

I stood up, taking his mug with me. I pottered around the room, plumping cushions, turning on a side lamp, straightening things. Then I opened a window a crack. Dad hated a draught, but the place was stuffy. It always had that slightly beefy edge to it, even now, which I used to attribute to mum's cooking. But that was long gone. Dad had mastered sausages, grilled bacon, a chopped ham sandwich – processed meats, basically – but he wasn't knocking up a casserole every Thursday. Unlike mum. Every single Thursday.

Vividly, I remembered sitting on the high kitchen stools, learning my times-tables or, later, completing algebra, and watching mum as she meandered around the room. She would open cupboards to retrieve things, glacé cherries and edible metal balls, like gems, for cakes – so fascinating to a child. Or intense little riches to drop into stews and soups: muslins of Bouquet Garni, silver cubes of stock powder. I had watched her, and I had learned. First from afar, and eventually by her side, stirring carefully as instructed, dropping things into pans – 'Not so high, darling, it will splash!'

I missed her.

When I had arrived to stay with dad, earlier this week, all that was in his fridge was a tub of margarine (almost gone), out-of-date marmalade and some squeezy cheese.

Dad never helped mum cook, not that I could remember anyway, except at Christmas when he made a song and dance about doing the goose. He would wrap the legs of the bird in layers of fat and foil, and he would score the surface of its breast deep, with large knives, and enthusiasm. It seemed to cook for hours, the smell starting early in the morning although we didn't ever eat before four. I always hated it, with its bitter, peculiar dark meat, but I loved the ritual.

And mum and dad would be confined to the kitchen together for once, bickering and laughing in equal measure. Dad would pinch mum on the bum whenever she went passed, and then feign innocence – and mum would flip him with the edge of her tea-towel, pretending to swat him if she thought he was coming too close. Eventually, the meal would be ready, and we would crowd around the table, a garden chair added to the mix, to accommodate Nana (though I always sat on it). The table would be massed with beautiful roast potatoes, jars of sauces - and sprouts, once verdant, now a dull seaweed green.

But then these memories distilled our history into a version of happy families. But we were not that: at least not just that. We were complex and unsettled in our story, meandering and detailed and loving, but bitter in places - and with unspoken folds of episodes that we did not dare to peek inside or unsettle.

On the surface, of course, I felt an immense warmth towards my dad, an affection wrapped in knotted shoe laces; tie-tying practice; model aeroplanes; a shared hatred of broccoli.

Broccoli. It always made me chuckle. Dad used to watch as I placed it in my mouth, watch as I then dropped it whole into my plastic tumbler, wink, and never say a word. Sometimes I even saw him spit his own broccoli into a handkerchief. I would giggle, and he would dramatically wave his hands around to shush me, eyes wide, mouth smirking. Looking back, of course, mum must have known.

But those were early days, and as short trousers and side partings dissolved into hair-gel, jeans and tight t-shirts, he began to move away from me. There was a shift, a colder shoulder. My music shifted to light pop, then angst-ridden ballads. My friends an alternative crowd, a mix of girls and boys. My dad, disapproving. Stoical. Silent.

By fifteen I knew for certain – admitted it to myself, I should say – and I felt sure that the world knew, too. My secret otherness was never discussed, and yet it was slashed across my body. I felt tattooed, marked, illuminated. Daubed. Obvious. It was a heady, terrifying sensation. And I wanted to share the load: to talk to dad, for him to turn back, towards me. To come back.

But he did not.

And like mum, with the broccoli, and the tumblers and the hankies, he knew. Of course, he knew. Yet mum pretended not to notice things because there was a joy in keeping the secret. There was a wink, and a warmth, and a smile. Dad pretended not to notice this because he thought there was dirt inside this secret. Filth. So, at first, I wanted him to acknowledge it because I was scared: but eventually, I wanted him to acknowledge it because I was angry.

He never did. Even when I told him, seventeen years old, my heart broken for the first time. Even then, smashed to smithereens, sobbing, limp, he gave me a half-hearted manly hug that turned into a slap across the shoulders - and then followed it with, 'Don't be silly, son. Don't be silly.'

Silly. Like a technicolour children's animation; a spilt drink; hidden vegetables; a pinch on the bum. Not like a ripe and perfectly-formed young heart, pulverised and fragmented. Not like fear and loneliness and confusion.

And then as time went on it was unspoken, this thing. Not mentioned. Whispers with mum in the kitchen sometimes, telling me 'not to mind dad,' saying he 'didn't understand these things'.

I got married. Paul was happy to go away for the ceremony – Vegas – flashing lights, night clubs and missing parents-in-law. I told him they would not want to come because of the travel, the flights. It was too far. In truth, getting married abroad was a salvation. Because I didn't think dad would have come anyway, but this way I didn't have to find out.

I talked about it openly, though, told them both we were marrying – I just never explicitly invited them. I recalled a Sunday lunchtime telling them about the hotel, how we had planned the service, and Mum smiled and nodded, did her best to ask a few questions. She had met Paul a few times and was not a prude, but this was alien for her. Still, she tried: so, I did not mind. But dad stared at his dinner plate for most of the meal, periodically made a 'humph!' noise quietly, or raised his eyebrows. At one point he even shook his head - I couldn't help it, incensed, I burst out, asking him what was the problem? But he said nothing.

I returned from the wedding, gave them a photo, and then it was never mentioned again.

A noise from the couch brought me back into the room, a little snort from dad. It was starting to get dark now, and tawny shadows fell through his faded, yellowing net curtains. The temperature was dropping. The movie we had been watching had given way to the news.

He grunted again, and his head jolted up and down. He unpeeled his lips and opened his eyes.

"Cold!" he barked.

I rushed over to the fan-light, still ajar. A child again, fearful that he would notice. That it would be my fault.

"What is it?" he said then, looking around him. "Where is it?"

"OK, dad?" I said, and went over to him, sat down next to him and tapped his knee. He reeled back from me, confused, lost. When he spoke again, he was quieter.

"Where am I?"

"You're home dad, it's just dark... wait a minute..."

I got up, slowly, and walked over to the standard lamp and switched it on. Then I went to the dining room and turned the overhead light on. The space opened up again, a shock even to me.

"Oh!" dad said. I wasn't sure if it was a happy sound or not.

"Shall we get you to the bedroom?"

He didn't answer, and continued to stare at the dining room, in awe. I took this as a yes, and an opportunity to move him while he seemed placated and cooperative. I walked back over to him, put one arm low behind him, to his waist, and pulled the top of his trousers slightly while I pushed into the small of his back. I wrapped my body close in a shadow of his and placed my other hand gently on his forearm. He acquiesced, leant forward – nose over toes – and pushed his dry, huge palms into his thighs, in an attempt to stand up.

It took a full two minutes before he was upright.

We shuffled together across the carpet and then the dining room floor, and made our way to his bedroom. As we walked, a chain of inanities dripped from my mouth, cotton wool words – I told him I would make him a cup of tea; I asked him if he had liked the film; I reminded him we had more bacon left for breakfast tomorrow. He did not speak. His breath bulged out of him in tufts and lumps, falling around us and in between my sentences, louder with each step.

As we entered the bedroom, he started to fiddle with the front of his pyjama bottoms, and peel away the fly. Too late, I realised what was happening and I tried ineffectually to steer him to the en-suite, tantalisingly close by. After a few seconds I stopped, gave up, and stood next to him in silent solidarity, while the pale arc of his sour urine sprayed onto the bedroom carpet.

"All done, dad?"

"All done," he said, as he covered himself up again.

"OK then," I said, "Let's get comfy."

I staggered him the last few metres to the bed and managed to seat him heavily on the edge. I left him balanced there as I went to get more nightwear, worried he might tumble or nod back to sleep as I did so. I managed to extricate him from most of his clothes but gave up on changing his vest, his arms skinny and bending as wings when I tried to mould them through the holes.

I grabbed the baby-wipes from the bedside cabinet.

"Mmm... No!" dad cried when he saw them.

"Come on," I coaxed, "You'll feel better afterwards."

I started to wipe his hands, and he allowed me to hold them and turn them, one at a time, slowly cleansing the webbed and mottled skin. It was bloated in places, sunken in others. The backs of his hands as orange segments: laced with knotted veins and tendons, visible through the surface. I swabbed his skin; the spaces between his heavy, hairy fingers. His nails were too long, I noted, ridged, corrugated. Dad sat, silently watching.

I pulled a new wipe from the pack and came towards his face, careful to ensure the wipe was in full view, that he knew what was coming. He didn't register it for a few seconds, and then lurched backwards.

"Mmmhhh... No! Go away," he cried.

"Come on, dad."

"Bugger off! Stupid sod."

It was his old voice, his old self. For a moment I stopped, and a quick laugh burst from me. I dropped my hand to the edge of the bed and looked at him, chuckling. Surprised, dad laughed too. We sat together inside the memory of this feeling for a moment. Then he leant forward slightly, and patted my hand.

"You're a good boy," he said.

I felt cold tears prick my eyes.

"Come on then, dad, let's get you settled, and I'll make that tea."

A few shuffles and 'humph!'s and manoeuvres later and he was propped up in bed. I should have changed the bedding while he slept that afternoon, I realised, but I plumped the pillows and pulled the sheets tight as best I could, with him swaddled inside.

There was an old portable television set in the room, a concave big-bellied screen with a huge base and rear. I had linked it up to a free satellite box a few months back. I found the sticky remote and turned it on, leaving it showing an antiques programme, then placed the remote by his side – in pretence that he could operate it.

"Right!" I called, "Tea."

I walked out the room, jumping the dark splatter on the carpet, and went to make us both a hot drink. While the kettle boiled, I searched under the sink for suitable cleaning products; I found some sort of spray, and a carpet talc of sorts – well beyond its sell-by date of course, but it smelt floral and couldn't be worse than what was there now.

I came back into the bedroom wearing pink rubber gloves and carrying two bottles and a sponge. Dad looked over, surprised.

"You still here?" he croaked.

I said nothing, and bent over the patch on the floor to begin scratching and spraying. As I did so, I glanced under the bed and saw clouds of dusty fluff collected around an old pair of slippers, and a bed pan. I needed to have words with the cleaners.

A few moments later, and I had replaced the cleaning goods and was walking back into dad's bedroom again, this time with some tea. Mine, in a large chipped, china mug – his in the plastic beaker that he hated so much. But he was already back asleep again.

I sat on the chair beside his bed. It was the first time I had been able to have a leisurely look around this room; it was dad's domain, and for years he had not even wanted me to come into it. The same pictures had adorned the walls for years, I realised. A cross-stitch hung above the bed, made by Nana if I remembered correctly: 'Bless this House' it said. On the wall opposite, was a framed clipping of dad from the local newspaper, after he won a fishing contest – a photo of him alongside the article, galoshes to his knees.

Placed on the table where the television sat there was a little porcelain hedgehog, but nothing else. It wasn't even facing the right way around.

I took another swig of tea and sat back, beginning to relax. Glancing to my right, I took in the bedside table beside me, woven rattan coasters, a side lamp, a framed picture of mum: the glass dirty and milky and the picture faded into browns.

Propped up against the wall, next to the image of mum, was a familiar photo album. I picked it up and started to flick through, as I drank my tea. Me and mum in bumper cars, when I was aged seven or eight; mum and dad standing on the doorstep of the house, looking proud – dad's moustache, a temporary mistake; mum sitting in a park in a summer dress, laughing into the camera; me, large tummied and pink shouldered, sitting on a beach next to an enormous sandcastle, aged about ten. Me again, in my school uniform on the first day of secondary school, blazer sleeves to the tips of my thumbs, chin jolted upwards in a grin.

Then there weren't many more of me; in fact, not much order to the collection at all after that. There were a few newspaper clippings – some, I wasn't sure why he had kept – and a few very old, loose photographs, Nana, Grandad, and other people I didn't know, the grey images jumbled amongst sepia newsprint and tangerine seventies snapshots.

I turned a page or two, but they were empty.

Dad snuffled, and I looked up. His eyes were open, watching. He was awake: I wondered how long he had been observing me. His skin was a puckered and dimpled grey - and I noticed with a shock that his lips had a dark-blue tinge. And yet that there was a hint of a soft smile there.

"OK, dad?" I asked, quietly.

"OK, son," he replied.

He closed his eyes again.

I waited a moment and then I leant forward and managed to rearrange his pillow, his position, until he was lying flatter in the bed. His arms lay outside the covers, still and straight. His head dropped back, his mouth slightly open.

I watched him for a moment, before I turned the album over in my hands. Then I looked through the book again. I looked through the book with fresh eyes - clean, unadulterated eyes. I brought the images close to my face in the half-light; I peeled back the ancient cellophane where I could, to retrieve and examine the snaps. I saw myself in my mum. I saw my dad in my Nana. I saw the things I remembered so clearly, and the things I had forgotten. Dad in the corner of the beach photo, his eye-line trained on me, joy in his face at the castle we had built, and at my delight. Mum's right hand on her left as she sat in the park, twisting her wedding ring as she did, for comfort, in habit, a dozen times a day. Me, my confidence, my faith in my dad and my world, going to big school with no cause for fear.

When I had finished, I rested the album back on the bedside table to the side of me, but turned my chair, just a little, to face my dad, in his bed, and rest my hand atop the book. I took a last look at the blurred and damaged image of my mum on the table. I kissed two fingers and tapped them on the sticky glass of the frame, and closed my eyes in rest.

A few hours later, he murmured and turned, his eyes half-open, but this time unseeing. I jolted upright, confused, alarmed for a moment, and scattered the album to the floor, its pages falling open, sepia and grey photos sprinkled like a crumbling moth. I jumped to catch the book, and as I did so, I knocked mum's photo flat. It dropped, face down, onto the table.

And there was my wedding photo, sellotaped clumsily in place, on the back of the frame.

Astonished, I dropped my hands into my lap and froze. And I felt like I had broken into a room I should not have entered. As if I was creeping around inside; I had stepped clumsily back inside a secret. I had no idea they had kept it. That he had it. And I had no idea how it came to be kept in such a precious place.

I looked over to dad. Bewildered.

He murmured again, louder this time, and then, of a sudden, the noise stopped.

He moved away. He started to move away.

"Dad?" I called - carefully, softly. I wanted to speak to him, to talk, to listen.

"Dad?" a little louder, as I leaned in towards him.

But there was no one there to answer me.

His oily eyes slid closed, and his body lay still, relieved. The dad I remembered, the dad I had forgotten: both of these people. All of them. They were all there. Yet none of them were there.

And then in a flicker, a tremor - on a shooting star - he was gone.

A Screech of Gulls

When he ran, he was sandblasted clean. He could feel the elements, their force against him - travelling through his hair, trying to squeeze into his eyes, ears, mouth. This was real, present. Corporeal.

Now, as he jogged along the beach, he swallowed the air, gulped this feeling, and revelled in the reassuring thump of his rucksack against his lower back. He took in, yet discounted, the odd sensation as it swung slightly too far to the left each time, the contents unsettled and uneven.

His feet bounced on the firm ground. Wet sand, as compacted salt, beneath him.

He loved this beach. He loved the lengthy, smooth path of ochre that he ran. To reach it, you had to clamber across many metres of ramshackle, irregular pebble and rock, strands, sometimes heaps of dried, black bladderwrack, husks of crabs and clams. It smelt sour, sharp. Briny. Perhaps this put some people off: it was rarely busy.

He continued to run, faster now. Faster than he would usually go. A screech of herring gulls lifted up from the ground in front of him and circled angrily above. The salt was buffering against his ears, cold and grey, the gulls' protests mingling with the whoosh of the breeze and waves.

Faster, and he could feel his knees again, feel the ball of his foot hit the sand. He was aware of his fingertips, the point of his nose, both white, yet almost steaming with cold. Dry ice.

In the distance, five minutes, perhaps eight minutes ahead of him, at the other end of the bay, he could see the little row of outlets on the headland. Here was the café he was heading to. Here, the pebble and stone finally gave way fully to the sand. No brackish weed lay there, and a row of tatty seaside shops, a post-box, a small carpark, bordered the beach and challenged nature. This was where a handful of tourists would come, and where locals sometimes sat for coffee, or breakfast.

He was going to meet Gemma.

The gulls continued to circle as he maintained his speed, though one lone crow remained, confidently, on the stones just ahead of him. Disdainful of him.

He did not know exactly what he was going to say, though it could be the last time they met. So goodbye, obviously, maybe, perhaps - but wrapped in what platitudes, he wasn't sure.

He ran faster, just slightly faster. Pushing himself to the edges of his abilities. Pushing his legs hard down so that his feet shattered the surface of the wet sand into honeycomb prints. He was angry with himself, frustrated, and tired. Enough. This was enough.

His rucksack swung erratically and clattered against his back; he was almost sprinting. Heavy panting breath hit the air, moist, visible. He could feel and taste the water's edge on his tongue: saline.

And what would she say in return? He had barely considered this. He had an image of her on arrival, and an image of himself leaving, and a glimpse of the feeling, just out of view, out of touch, of the relief he would have afterward. But he could see very little in between. Was avoiding considering it, he supposed: all the different ways the conversation might go.

He ran near to the water, closer than he would usually go. The small, delicate lace of the retreating waves lapped close to his feet. His trainers were sinking, the sand collapsing slightly under his weight, where it was sodden and fresh from the sea. This slowed him down again.

He had only been seeing Gemma for a little over six months. Only really got to know her for the last four or five. She was light, airy – always giggling, upbeat. It left him dizzy when he left her. He was thrown into a patch of stars, a scattering of glitter, of hope, sparkles when they spoke. It was so far removed from his daily life, grind, grey, normality, that it was infectious. Addictive.

But secret. And wrong.

He was almost there, so he started to wind back towards the land, taking a tortuous route across the shingle that came between the water and the buildings. The sounds shifted from hollow wind, and water, to snippets of cars, young children – laughter, even. They got louder as he approached. He slowed his pace, jogging again, then bounding, then stepping - until he was walking.

He climbed the metal stairs; green paint peeled off onto his hands in tiny splinters as he held the rails. He stopped on the concrete footpath at the top and paused – stretched out his limbs in his little ritual of movements, counting in his head as he did so, noting his bag sliding from one side to the other. He started a second round of stretches then thought better of it – knew he was delaying the inevitable.

He walked towards the café – spotted Gemma straight away, sat outside at a wooden bench, holding a glass coffee cup in her right hand. She was looking straight ahead, not at him. Her profile distinct in the sunlight; she was sat straight, face serious. Noble.

She did not turn as he approached, even after the point when she must have sensed him, when he felt sure she must have heard him, known he was there. She waited until he put his bag down on the bench, then, deliberately, she turned to face him.

She had been crying, he saw.

"Hi," she said.

"Hi!" he replied. Too upbeat.

"Sit down,"

"Umm… I don't…" he stuttered back. He was not used to her being so serious, assertive.

"Sit down," she instructed.

He didn't reply but pushed his bag along the bench, and sat awkwardly, propped on the corner, not wanting, or deserving, perhaps, to be at ease.

"Well?" she asked, eyebrows low.

She was looking just to his left – face tilted up towards him but eye contact missing, a little off centre. Less confident than she pretended, he realised.

He gave a little shrug. Felt wholly useless, pathetic. There was a silent pause.

"Do you want something? Coffee?... I got this. But I don't know why. I can't eat it."

She shoved a little, pink plate towards him, on it a muffin, swaddled in black, waxy paper. Dutifully, without thinking, he picked it up and started to unpeel it from its shell. He bit into it, a hearty bite, glad to have a reason not to speak. The chocolate was pickled by the salt on his lips. He ate it anyway.

"You asked me here," she stated.

He stopped. Put the muffin down and licked his lips.

"Annie knows," he said. The words popped out like two little stones. Polished and hard.

"Oh," she said. She looked down into her lap. "So, what now?"

"I don't know," he said, "But I can't do this… for now, at least. I need some time to chat to her. She needs some time to figure things out. You know."

"OK"

"I'm sorry," he said, with a hint of a request, pleading in his tone. "I am sorry," he tried again.

Neither of them spoke, and as they sat in silence the chatter and clatter seemed to rise up around them and fill the gap, the space. He could not hear the beach. They stayed still for two, perhaps three full minutes.

"You should have told her about me when I first found you," she stated, eventually.

"I know."

"I did tell you to."

"Yes," he said, flat, quiet. "You did."

"So, how come she knows? You told her?"

She looked up at him, this time into his eyes. She had her mother's dark hair, certainly looked like her - but he fancied she had a hint of him about her, a rumour of him, his genes, in her nose, in her eyes perhaps.

"She… she saw your picture on my phone."

"What… An accident?" another pause, "Were you ever actually going to tell her about me? I mean, would you have told her, if she hadn't caught you out?"

"Yes... I… eventually, I would have. But I wanted to find the right time. It's not easy you know. It's not easy for me."

She snorted.

"It's not easy for you?" she said, angry now. "I'm fifteen, remember. I'm the child. Not you. Me. I'm the one who never had a dad. I'm the one whose dad has turned out to be a… to be…"

"What?" he snapped.

"A coward."

They sat still again, her raw anger palpable, pumping the air around them into its own pulse. She was turned away from him. Pink in the face. No sparkles.

"Sam heard her," he said, almost to himself, "He heard her shouting. About you. He knows. I don't know how to explain it to him."

"Well, good luck," she said, almost shouting, voice tremoring.

The words were skewered through their centre, with rage. He should not have mentioned Sam. It was insensitive, he realised. Of course, it was.

"I don't know what to do," he replied, quietly.

"I'm going," she said. And stood up.

A feeling of panic settled on his chest, pricked his skin.

"Bye," and she turned and walked away. Just like that.

She walked away towards the noise of the cars and the children, towards the land. She left him sitting on the bench, with his bag, picturing Sam, Annie. Picturing his parents, friends, the disappointment. The shock. Shame. Picturing his old, grey life. A blank one before him, empty. Picturing Gemma laughing, giddy. Angry. Absent. The images flickered in and out of view: a strobe.

He had thought for a split-second he would follow her, but he had waited just a little too long, and the moment was gone, and she was gone, and he was alone. And it was real.

A squall of wind carried the sound of the herring gulls towards him, hit his ear with a mist of silt and sodium.

It was real.

He stood, and looked out towards the shoreline, back towards the tawny sand, the lumps of knotted weed, the loops of irascible birds, swooping a few metres above ground.

Then he grabbed his bag, with its uneven contents, its lumps, bumps – a pair of shoes, some underwear, a book, a phone, a wallet – his passport. He grabbed his bag and swung it across his shoulders until it settled to one side.

And then he ran.

Jessica Was Nice

Jessica was surprised at the number of people who turned up to her funeral. Pleasantly surprised. Lou and Adam; Caroline; Sam; even Mr. Bradshaw her old neighbour was there to see her off. It was quite touching - though unsettling. Why had they come? Was it simply because they had liked her?

Yet it seemed odd, if you liked someone, to visit them after their passing rather than before.

The truth was, she knew she had been popular. She had made a point of being as nice as possible (or as nice as was reasonable, at least) to everyone. Were they there to look righteous, respectful? To try to match her virtuosity? For show, perhaps?

Look at me! They were saying - I was friends with a good and popular woman! Perhaps some of this will end up staying with me if I attend her funeral, dusting me with microscopic beads of integrity, by association.

Or perhaps it was to gawk – to be a part of a spectacle. That seemed, sadly, to be a logical explanation, given the nature of her death. These people were rubbernecking at the gallows; stretching out to try to see above the heads of others, to get a better view, closer to the story, the action. They wanted the inside gen, to see inside the story.

To be inside the story.

Outside the church, it was a clear, spring morning. The sun was warm, but the air was chilled. It was a day perfectly constructed for gentle activities: for picnics, strolls, dog walking. But funerals? No. This was an insult to the spring bulbs and blue sky.

Mind you, Jess noted, people were not in black. They wore an array, a maelstrom of colours. Mr. Bradshaw was in blue. Jennifer Hamby wore a striped dress, of all things, with splashes of teal, pink; two-toned: a stick of rock. Lou had a black coat on, at least, but underneath Jess caught a flash of a red dress as she walked.

This was obviously by design. Clearly, they had been told not to wear funeral garb. Yet Jessica had not once expressed a wish for this. She did, she gathered, have a reputation for being chipper, smiley. So - they assumed she would like this. But no, she did not. It seemed somewhat obscene.

Dress code: disrespectful.

All the effort she put into having people like and admire her – which had sometimes taken a good deal of patience - seemed wasted. What was the point, if people weren't even going to take your death seriously?

They were moving inside now, clenching hymn sheets and teeth as they approached the pews. They lowered their voices though continued to talk, she noticed. She saw Caroline again, leaning in, to whisper to someone she didn't recognise, lifting an Order of Service in front of her face as if to hide the fact she was still gabbling away. She never did know when to shut up. Jessica smiled though, while she watched this, as was her habit, even now it seemed.

The church was full, just the front rows empty and awaiting her family. Jessica looked around for Helen: eventually spotted her towards the back, in the middle of a row. Not pride of place, no recognition of her importance. A nobody's seat. A nothing.

Helen was misplaced, small. She had lost weight in the ten days since Jessica had seen her. She was dressed in a navy blouse, with tiny white polka-dots. She had tied her hair up in a sort of bun, and was wearing red lipstick, striking against her dark skin - though it was already starting to fade. Of course. Ha! If she had been able to talk to her, she would have leaned in, passed her lipstick of her own, and a mirror, without saying a word. These were the things that she did for people, before she died. This was why people liked her.

Helen looked smart, put together, and dreadful. Paler, dry, shivery. Jessica wanted to be with her, to talk to her old friend again. To comfort her, or even just to chat about the mundane, the silly, the superficial. But she could not.

Now the organ started, and the congregation shuffled to its feet. She watched the pall bearers carry her coffin over the threshold; behind them, approaching, James, and Paul and John. James, at the lead, looking straight ahead, at the back of the coffin. Paul looking up and out, around him, at his audience, the congregation. John, though, kept his head down, the tip of his red, damp nose just visible.

She had wanted to be cremated.

They walked the slow path towards the front of the church and she came around behind them and followed suit, marvelling that they had chosen this hymn – Abide With Me – which she had sat through for both her parents' funerals. What would have brought them to do this? And how did this fit with the bright, cheerful clothes everyone wore? It seemed ludicrous – a group of adults in party clothes, in an old church, singing what was quite possibly the melancholiest song on record. The epitome of morose. I mean seriously, who had coordinated this thing?

She thought back to her mother's funeral. She couldn't help it. And with the memory she became that husk again, that tiny, empty thing she had been for weeks around the time of her mother's death.

She had barely been able to stand at the funeral, and had walked between James and John. James had pulled her up and on, his arm too stiff, too high – his grip too hard. John had leant into her, whispered in her ear, soft sounds amidst the hard clacking of the shoes on stone. He did this all the way up the aisle, until eventually she felt his warmth on her skin, permeating the dullness that had overtaken the rest of her body. For days beforehand, she had been cold. Days.

She had never forgotten this. Never forgotten his quiet strength; his innate kindness; his pure warmth.

James had been somewhat brusque with her all day, embarrassed by her uncharacteristic rawness. And that was the start of it: a burgeoning desire to be free of him, away. It was planted that day as a little seed. And slowly, inside of her, it had grown. A little bean-shoot, that no one else could see - but it was there. And no one had ever known. Ever. Not even Helen.

She remembered the wake, at a local hotel bar. She felt proud, in fact, looking back, that she had managed to hold it together as much as she did. Circulating the room, she had chatted to most people there, chatted through sniffs and a dry mouth, asking them if they wanted another drink and how they were getting home and where they were staying and how they were feeling. She was treading water. Asking them a series of platitudes, and nodding and prompting as she often did, while saying very little herself. This was a skill she had learnt, her knack – though not something that had come naturally. She had practised. It took work. Until, for some time now, she had been able to lull people into believing her a friendly, lovely person, while really saying nothing at all. Perhaps that was it, why so many people were here.

They thought they knew her.

James, on the other hand, told people he was a good person, often. Some believed him, with his subtle brags and illustrations of wholesome, wholegrain virtuousness. Charity marathons, that sort of thing. Yet, of course, it was not enough to say the thing. He needed to be the thing: scratch the surface, and he was not. He was a mass of neuroses and cruelty. Neurotic cruelty that he lashed out on a daily basis to Jessica.

Example one: he was home every Friday night by 5.30. He made sure to be out the door of work by 4.45, made sure to come home as quickly as possible. He worked long, hard hours, Monday to Thursday, and then he clocked off at quarter to five, Friday. Every. Single. Time.

Except the occasion when she had asked him to come to meet Paul's A-Level Physics teacher. The school had called; it did not sound good, she told him. Something about an incident and Paul swearing and standing up to the teacher in front of the whole class (like the cocky shit he was, she thought). Yet that was the one evening, for some reason, James had to stay on late and finish a project. So yes, he finished at 4.45 every Friday – except when she had actually needed him.

Example two: James would get roaring, aggressively, disgustingly drunk about every four or five months. Once, he had even spat in her face.

Ok, so perhaps she should have led with that example first.

You get the drift.

Anyway, now there they were, her three men, about to sit at the front of the church. Dressed in dark suits at least, but with daffodils as button holes. She hated daffodils. And then there was talking. Well, a scripture reading, actually. Jessica did what she always did now, during religious readings or prayers, and said the alphabet while wearing a Mona Lisa smile.

She used to be religious, and she supposed everyone believed she still was. Hence, well - this. But no. That boat sailed when she first got sick, around nine years ago. It was so close on the back of her mum dying, that it seemed utterly incredible. She could not believe they were right, in what they were telling her. No one could possibly have this much shit in one year. But they were: they were right.

For a while she still believed in God, she clung onto her faith by the tips of her fingers - but they were fingers curled around a door frame, curled around a door that was being slowly squeezed shut. If He had any control over what was happening, then He really was a callous bastard. So, for a while she believed in Him, but hated Him. Then she stopped caring what He thought, or what she thought of Him, and forgot Him. Moved on.

But she didn't explicitly mention that to people. It would be awkward, and she didn't want anyone to think less of her. She carried on going to church, just sometimes, every now and then. And she gave up chocolate for Lent and bought religious Christmas cards instead of jokey ones. It seemed this was all it took for people to assume she had a faith.

"Let us pray," the priest said.

People sort of shuffled, unsure whether to kneel or bow their heads.

It was a generic prayer, not very imaginative. She wondered if James had contributed anything at all to this event.

And then the priest spoke again, briefly, about what she was like. Jessica wanted to laugh, having never met him before and all, but she did not. She heard him describe her as measured, dependable, and 'above all, kind.' So, that was worth listening to, really.

He called up Paul for the eulogy. Of course, Paul would do the eulogy. As he stepped out of the pew his father slapped him on his back twice - as if he were going off to the bar for the last round - and then he was striding up, long-limbed, loose, ready. Around her, people smiled and nodded at each other: they were ready for an amusing and confident little speech. They were ready to be entertained. They needed an interlude, and Paul would not let them down. He was the golden child – a cheeky chappy who might be a little rough around the edges, but was warm and smooth at his core.

His handsome face settled itself into a resigned half smile – a smile with the corners of his mouth turned down, if there was such a thing. He waited. He held them enthralled.

Jessica held a terrible secret.

She could never stand him.

Even as a toddler. She had always felt, somehow, like he did everything on purpose, to test her. Two nights after she brought him home from hospital, she was convinced he was evil, demented, when he cried and searched for feeding at her breast all night. Suckled, was sick – projectile milky sick – and then wanted feeding again.

And after that, every night he woke at least twice - for five long, listless years. Without fail. That took quite some commitment. You see?

Every morning he ran away when it was time to get dressed.

And every evening he managed to tip half of his food onto the floor, when he ate.

But everyone adored him – with his blonde hair and one dimpled grin. He was fast to learn and quick to talk. He ran just a week after he could walk. Incredible. And he was joyous, loved life. Giggled constantly.

She had never trusted men who laughed out loud.

Now, he was talking, using a whole paragraph of adjectives to describe her, while around her, people sniffed and nodded. Dependable; charismatic; charming; captivating; kind. And among all those hard syllables and sounds he still managed to slip in easy tones, and softness. He told a tale – one with very little narrative – of how he and his brother had gone out once, into the field near the house, and had wandered too far, gone into the woods. How they had been lost, and John had cried but he had comforted him, as the older brother. But he was not scared, no, he would never be scared, because he knew his mum would always be there to rescue him.

All around, people continued nodding and smiling. He saw Lou slip her head tenderly to one side until it almost sat fully on Adam's shoulder. Adam too, wet eyed, and yet doe-eyed.

Rescue him: of course, she had been there to rescue him. She had bailed him out dozens of times, emotionally, practically and financially. He always came to her, and she always did it. Yet here he was, a glamourous figure at the pulpit. Like he could do no wrong. Like he was the hero.

He had finished, and there was another prayer, and then a 'musical interlude' – an organ piece. (What were they thinking?) and everyone sat awkwardly in an almost silence while they listened.

Then, thank goodness, it was over. They all stood while the organist began, haltingly, the opening notes to 'All Things Bright and Beautiful' – the priest said chosen by her sons, as they remembered her watching them perform it in a school show for her. (She did not remember watching them perform it in a school show for her.) Then they stepped out of the front pew and into the aisle and started the march back out towards the door, the whole mood of the congregation walking the tightrope of the discordant sounds balanced precariously across a jovial tune. James, serious, slightly red in the face. Paul, glassy eyed but smiling and gently shaking his head, stopping as he went down the aisle, often, to give a quick two-handed shake to various men he saw along the way.

People started to chatter over the last bars of the music and she could hear, all around her, choked voices commenting on how lovely it was: how lovely she was, and therefore how fitting the morning had been. 'So Jessica', someone had said.

There was a swell of people trying to exit the church and eventually, when she reached the door, she found this was because James and Paul were right at the exit, hardly even outside, chatting to people, shaking more hands. James was telling everyone how proud he was of Paul, and how Jessica would have been proud, too. And people were saying that there really only was one Jessica, she was remarkable, unique; we will never, ever forget her. She was already an angel, even when she was on the Earth.

John had stepped away, at least two metres to the left of them. He was crying, clenching one fist and dabbing his face with the other, swaddled in ripped tissue. Helen was talking to him, one hand placed on his shoulder, face leaning in. His father had barely acknowledged him throughout the whole thing, barely registered him even, would be tuning him out now, with his tears and his veracity. James had always thought John a little dull, a little weak, a little embarrassing.

Yes, James was strong; Paul was clever; John was weak; Jessica was nice.

Well, Jessica thought, she couldn't wait to see their faces when the Will was read.

Change

She smiled a soft and subtle smile as she approached the counter.

At the till, the young man continued wiping the same spot repeatedly, circles of bleach and frustration. Not much more than 25, 26, deep lines were clenched along his forehead and between his eyebrows, swollen from annoyance and lack of sleep.

But he was kind, you could see this, he was kind. And he was good. And he was sad.

"There you go," she said, as she placed her almost empty mug on the counter, before him.

He looked up. Paused, still in thought.

"Can I pay you?" she said.

"Hey, thanks," he replied, and genuine appreciation flickered across his face as he registered the mug. "That'll be £1.20," he said.

He turned his back on her to punch buttons on the till. She noted a harmonica poking out from the top of the pocket of jeans, barely visible.

She placed the £1.20 on the counter and stood still, rubbing one more coin between finger and thumb until she could feel friction and static; until she could feel the metal begin to warm up.

He took the change from the counter and picked up the cloth to go back to his cleaning.

"Thanks a lot; have a great day," he said, quietly. No eye contact; distracted again.

"This is for you," she stated. He looked up again.

She lifted her arm up high, and straight, and confidently. She held the coin delicately but securely between her right finger and thumb and cupped her left hand below it, to catch it should it fall. Like it was breakable; delicate.

Like it was precious.

He stopped, arched one eyebrow artfully.

"What's this?" he said.

"A little help," she answered, and smiled.

He took the coin from her, and stared down at it in his hand, confused.

"This is too much," he muttered, "It's practically as much as you paid for the coffee."

But she said nothing, and for a moment they stood in the peace of the still and the warmth; each looking at the other with a gentle smile. Then he slipped the coin into the back pocket of his jeans, so that in her mind's eye she saw and felt him push the coin alongside the harmonica until it reached the bottom of the pocket, securely; nudging and sliding it down like a penny in an arcade machine.

She turned away slowly and walked back towards the door.

****

If you were to ask Tim how he felt about his music, he would tell you that his music was a child sitting at a desk, waiting, staring out the window onto summer. His music was a child, an infant, waiting to be allowed down and free and outside, to play under the sunbeams. To play.

Because it was there, always, but squashed and frustrated. Shackled. It was not free.

And he did not 'play'. He worked. Even when he gigged, he worked. Because this was not truly a man making music - this was a grown up, paying the bills.

But nobody ever asked him, so he did not say this, and he continued on in this way.

Coffee shop by day – gig by evening – black dread by night.

Today, like any other, he had done a shift in the café, and like pretty much every other day he had wondered if he should just call it quits and give up on this ridiculous dream. What self-respecting 27-year-old man continues to think he can make a career from music? Continues to take home less than 20K a year?

The café had been quiet, and that made it worse. Tim had fallen deep into thought and one after another his fears and terrors had crept out from the boxes where he locked them down. And he had allowed this, he had indulged this. One after another, the boxes split open and the anxieties crept out until they flooded his mind and spilt out into the space around him.

He had another gig tonight, but he wasn't sure he could do it anymore. Another gig with The Jazz Hands, playing blues and jazz standards with his mediocre bandmates to a lacklustre audience. When he had first started doing this, he had been excited, regarding it as paying his dues – a tithe. But now, four years later, it seemed this was all there was. This was it.

Luckily, an elderly lady had come to the counter and with a jolt he was back in the room. After she had tipped him, generously, and gone, he had told himself that he'd give it another six months but do it properly this time – try harder. He must try harder.

But then something wonderful happened. He finished his shift and checked his messages, and there it was: an email asking him back after an audition. A promising email. With a real blues band. Professionals.

He was over the moon.

He told himself he'd enjoy himself at tonight's gig, he'd commit, he'd appreciate it, and not be such a bloody snob. It wasn't going to be for much longer.

This could be the start of something amazing.

****

Jenny's dad could always manage to bring her down. Every time she dared to voice an idea, a thought, a wish, he could somehow find a way to reshape it as a farcical fantasy. Stolen dreams. He was a pickpocket. She didn't know why she ever shared anything with him, yet each time she hoped, naively, it might be different.

She stood behind the bar and replayed the conversation they'd had today, in her mind. It was fresh and painful. A tender bruise.

He was probably right. How would she afford to go to college? Wasn't she too old? And what university would ever take her? She didn't even have a full set of A levels; had never passed her maths; had a recent CV that included nothing more salubrious than a brief stint as a supermarket supervisor and several years working behind the bar of The Jazz Club.

She was now such a fixture in the place that she managed to move through the motions of serving one of the musicians a whole round of drinks while on automatic pilot.

This stark reflection on her life made her feel bare. Naked. And she didn't like what she saw.

"Keep the change," the guy said, as she passed him over his last pint. He was here every week but had never tipped her before. They smiled at each other.

She slipped the coppers into the charity box but dropped the larger coin into her apron pocket. What the hell.

The coin slid down and then settled comfortably and surprisingly heavy at the bottom of her apron.

And then she stopped. And thought. He had scoffed at her, made fun at her credentials - but then, wasn't that exactly why she wanted to go back to education in the first place? To change all that? To write herself a new history?

She paused. Dad was grown from bitterness and regret. But she was not. Not yet.

She was going to do this.

****

Dayna rubbed and twisted her engagement ring ferociously. She sat alone at the table and let the sound of the harmonica drench into her body, swell the blood in her veins and her ears.

This had not been a good day.

She was unsure how long she had been sat here, drinking, crying, alone. But it must have been at least an hour – she hoped longer, as she could see in front of her that there was already a collection of three empty wine glasses.

She was still shaking. It could not be real. It did not seem real. The image she had of Joe with that girl, that girl in the café, the pair of them holding hands, leaning in, laughing. The image that settled into focus as she got even closer, of his hands, hands in her hands, his thumb rubbing the back of hers, gently. Tenderly.

No. This could not be real.

Joe had been her saviour and now he was her Judas. It was hard to fathom. He had looked after her, his protection encompassed her and sheltered her, and she had thought they would stay there together for ever. She would stay in his shelter, under the olive tree, out of the heat of the sun. But now she was exposed.

She thought her skin would be seared from her bones.

None of this made any sense.

She was going to call him. Work it out. She knew she could be difficult; had been difficult. All her life she had struggled with men. This must be salvageable. But she didn't even have her bloody phone with her. It was out in the car, and that seemed such a very long way away now.

She downed the remains of her fourth glass of wine, and unsteadily, carefully, stood up slowly, to walk towards the bar. There was an old public phone out in the foyer, she knew.

All she needed was change.

She waited, patiently, while the barmaid chatted to another customer, her giddy laugh pinching and floating across the air as a butterfly, until she finished and turned towards Dayna, a smile still hovering on her lips.

"How can I help you?" she asked.

Dayna watched her face flicker and alter as she took in the smudged make-up under her bloodshot eyes.

"Can you change this note for some coins?"

"Sure," she said, and began to rummage in her apron pocket.

Dayna watched her pull out bits of paper, a hairband, some notes, and finally some coins. She counted them out, dropping them carefully from one hand to another, and then eventually letting them fall from her hand, into Dayna's. They felt surprisingly solid and warm against her palm. Heavy.

"Thank you," Dayna said.

The woman behind the bar closed her fingers around hers. They stood for a moment with their hands knotted together, as if holding something precious.

"You're welcome," she said.

As the barmaid turned her back on her, to go back to her work, Dayna stood there, with the warm coins pressing into her palm. A thought flitted through her mind.

She walked back across the room, passed the table where she had been sat, and dropped the coins into the pint glass on the stage, at the foot of the harmonica player. They took a while to settle, and clattered loudly, heavily enough to be heard over the band. She did this despite the fear. And she felt better for it.

****

She smiled a soft and subtle smile as she approached the counter. It was a little over a week later, and already the weather was changing, the sun sat higher in the sky making the light sharp, crisp. She waited patiently to place her mug on the counter.

"So, then; good luck," someone was saying – she assumed the manager, or supervisor perhaps.

"Cheers, mate," the young man was smiling, "I appreciate it."

"I can't believe you're leaving me alone!" his boss replied, mock tearful, lifting his hands to his face in a show of woe.

"I'm going to take one for the road though," the young man said, as he reached towards the coffee machine and then banged the warm, wet coffee grinds into a metal tray, "And I'm paying, for once!"

He pressed a button on the till and then dropped two coins in.

"What do you mean, for once?"

They both laughed, and then the manager finally registered her presence at the counter.

"Sorry love," he said, gently, "Did you want the bill?"

"£1.20?" she asked, passing him a note.

The till was still open, and the manager leant forward to scrape some coins from the plastic tray. As he did so, he leant across to his colleague.

"Seriously, though," he said, quietly to the young man, leaning into him, over his shoulder, with familiarity - coins still in hand, "You're an inspiration. I'm jealous, mate. I wish I had your guts."

He turned back around to face her and placed the coins on a saucer in front of her. She picked them up, carefully, one at a time, and placed them slowly into her purse.

A little help, she thought; everyone needs a little help sometimes.

She took the last coin and rubbed it, softly, until she could feel friction and static.

"Keep the change," she said, as she dropped it back onto the saucer.

She Walks Through Mud

She walks through mud to find you: feet squashed into woollen socks, into rubber boots. Her toes are swaddled tight, fashioned in a nest. She takes comfort in the pressure of the layers, fighting each other for space. Comfort amidst the chaos of your absence.

Across the field behind the house, she is searching. Determination in her stride, she is up to the hilt in splatters but does not care. She will find you.

Trudging through brittle leaves, sticks, moss - on she goes. Searching, her heavy stride making a mockery of nature; turning the brown and green around her into an electrical wire: a crackle, a snap, before the sludge beneath the fire swallows the noise.

She walks through mud to find you; heart recalibrated into a mouse beat, a bird beat - tremoring, racing beneath clothes and skin. Excitement, fear. Maybe you will be there, just ahead, around this bend. Maybe.

Her heavy, hot breath quickens, captures the cold into clouds.

Too scared to hear the lack of echo, she doesn't call your name. Fearful that you are not there, amidst the crackles, the moss. Yet on she walks, through mud; pellets sticking to legs, shrapnel glued to boots, cold cheeks, damp head beneath acrylic hat, fingers turned hard, stiff, white.

She walks, as the sun begins to dim. Around the bend, a loop, retracing steps. Looking closely now, in desperation. Looking at footprints, mess: artificial debris exciting her each time – a tissue, a wrapper, a plastic bag.

But they are not yours.

Back towards the house, and dual feelings of resignation and frustration jostle within her. She almost found you this time - almost saw you, she knows.

She almost conjured you, amidst the mud and electricity, and the memory of the walks you used to have.

The Mirror

6:30 pm

It did not matter that it was a Friday night, Mum said I had to go to bed at 7 o'clock, anyway.
She had people coming around.
She was sitting at her table, putting earrings in, and looking at me, through the me that was in the mirror. Her earrings were so long and dangly they were almost touching the freckly bits on her shoulders. They were like the tassels on grandma's curtains, only gold; I wanted to touch them. They looked like they would feel like tickles on my hand.
"Can I leave my light on and read?" I asked, looking at the back of her neck, because the 'me in the mirror' thing felt a bit weird.
She paused.
"I tell you what," she said, in a strangely quiet and deep voice, not her voice, "if you're a good boy, we can move the T.V. from the spare room into yours for the night. You can watch a film."
I reached one hand out and stroked the earring, and let it fall through my fingers like water. It felt disappointingly warm and stiff. But I didn't stop.
"Your neck is really white," I said.
"Wouldn't you like that?" she asked me, turning around to face me, pushing my hand away from the jewellery as if she was irritated with my fiddling, as usual. She smelt strong, like sponge cake. And shower gel.
"Yes, please," I said, but I wondered what I had to do, to show that I was good.
Mum turned back around to the mirror, so I sat on the edge of the bed really quiet and still and straight and not talking, because I knew she would make me leave if I was annoying.

She had stuck her hair up on top of her head. Usually she had hair falling all the way down her back and that's why I don't get to see her neck very often. But she had made it stay up with hairpins and things and it was a big pile of little curls fluttering on her head every time she moved. I wondered if she had done it to make it easier to put her earrings in. She didn't usually wear big earrings.

She stopped still and put her hands on her knees. For a second, she locked eyes with herself - like she was cross and going to tell her mirror-self off - and then she shut her eyes, tight, and took a slow, very deep breath, twice. One, two. I felt nervous all of a sudden, wondering if I had done something.

She opened her eyes again and smiled at mirror-me.

"How do I look?" she said, and turned around again, standing up, holding her dress out to the sides so I could see through the top layer of the fabric, see the shiny black fabric underneath. I didn't know there were two bits of fabric there. Why did they give her skirt two types of fabric?

I considered her question carefully and looked her over, seriously. She didn't usually look this way. It felt strange, and I didn't know if I liked it or not. And I liked that she had asked me, but I didn't know how to answer.

"Very pretty, but you'll look better when you've finished your hair." I said.

She did one of those big bursts of laughter she does when she snorts a bit like she's snoring. But then she surprised me because she carried on laughing, a little singing laugh, for a long time, leaning over like you would do when you are coughing too much to breathe, but she wasn't coughing, she was laughing, laughing like I haven't see her laugh in ages, so it made me laugh, too. I felt it start unexpectedly, like a giggle in my belly that crept out of my mouth without my permission, so I put my hand over my mouth to stop it, but it kept creeping out through my fingers. So, Mum and I were both laughing together. And it felt lovely and warm. And it felt like a memory.

6:50 pm

I could feel that the hair on the back of my head was a bit wet still, from the shower. Every now and then little trickles of water fell down like an army of ants. It was creepy, so I rubbed my head hard from side to side on the pillow really fast, to make it go away.
"What on earth are you doing?" Mum said, irritated, so I stopped.
She was standing in the middle of my room, squinting at a remote control, trying to get the DVD player to work. The light from my lamp made strange patterns across the floor, like bits of glass, and her skirt was lit up brightly, but a shadow fell across the bottom of her legs. Like she had no feet. Like she was floating.
"Do you want me to help, Mum?" I asked. I could see what she was doing wrong.
She threw the remote on my bed, but she didn't look annoyed.
"I have to finish the starters," she muttered.
She leant down and kissed me on the forehead. Her necklace fell onto my chin and then slipped across my cheek as she straightened up again, cold.
"Night, monkey," she said.
"Night," I said, and wrinkled up my nose at her and her silly nickname.

7:30 pm

Mum was playing her old-fashioned music with saxophones and ladies singing about moonlight and love when the doorbell rang. I heard her scamper down the hallway to open up, and then I couldn't quite hear what she said but the man on the other side of the door gave a really loud, sudden laugh, that sounded hot and big, and made me feel strange; then they both hissed and giggled when she tried to shush him again. He must have come in, because I heard the door shut and the noise of the cars and wind was trapped outside.

7:44 pm

Uncle Tim arrived. I knew it was him because of that special ring he does and the way he calls "Wahayyyy!" when you open the door. I wanted to go down to see him, but I couldn't because Mum had made it clear I was not to go downstairs on any account or under any circumstances, whatsoever.

I snuggled down deeper under the bedcovers and curled my body into a bean shape. The TV screen looked sideways, but it was surprisingly comfortable, and safe, even with my neck twisted around in a funny position. I scrunched up against my cuddly dinosaur, tightly. I pinned the duvet down around me and I felt like I was in a giant sock; like a giant bean, in a giant pod.

8:10 pm

I tried to focus on the film, but it was hard. I was picking at the corner of my duvet and saying my six times table to myself, when someone appeared in my doorway.

"Uncle Tim!" I cried.

The fact that it was late, and the weekend, and I had to stay upstairs - but he was standing in my room anyway - made it all much more exciting than it would normally be.

He came over to the bed, grinning. He was a tall, thin man with a long, pointed face, like an elbow.

"I'm not allowed downstairs," I stated.

"What you watching?" he asked, as he came over and sat on the edge of my bed. He faced the screen,

"Uh. Cool," he said.

I didn't think he knew the film, but he said it anyway, just to be kind. He was like that.

"Does Mum know you're in here?" I asked him. I could smell him and taste him like cold air.

"Cheeky fag," he said, as he leaned in to me.

I wasn't sure what he meant, but I giggled because he winked at me and used that voice he sometimes uses when he acts like we're in a gang together; when he acts like we're mates.

"Is Aunty Lynn here, too?" I asked.

"Sure is, bud," he winked again. "I'll try to get her to sneak past the armed guards too, if you like, but she's less likely to resist than I am so I wouldn't hold your breath."

"No," I said, but his words were like a tangled ball of knotted wool in my head and I couldn't untousle them to understand their meaning - though I felt disappointed, because it didn't sound like I would be getting any more visitors soon.

8:51 pm

The music was still playing, but everyone had moved to the kitchen and shut the door, and the front doorbell had been ringing for a really long time. I felt a little nervous sickness in my stomach as I tried to decide what to do. I didn't want to leave someone outside, but I knew I wasn't meant to go downstairs. The bell rang repeatedly like a miniature scream, and every time it made me flinch, even though I was expecting it. It was like I could feel the noise on my skin, on my arms and cheeks. I wanted it to stop.

"Mum!" I called, "Muuum!"

I was nervous, and it sounded weird – like a loud voice trapped inside a quiet voice. Like a loud voice with no volume.

"Mum!" I said loudly and quickly.

I listened for the sound of the kitchen door opening, and her feet, but the sounds didn't come. I slipped out of bed and put my slippers and dressing gown on. The doorbell was still ringing, loud angry rings, quick loud rings now, so I took a deep breath and went out to the top of the stairs.

From the top of the staircase I could see the front door and a dark shadow through the stained glass at the top. Mum had stripped all the paint off the door a few months ago and I didn't like it; I thought it looked like it wasn't a finished house anymore, like we were going backwards and had only just moved in, instead of just settling down. Someone was banging on the door now, banging and ringing the bell. I started to walk down the stairs. It was only when I got halfway down that I realised I was still holding my dinosaur.

I reached up and opened the latch on the door.

"Where is he?" the woman said, looking straight past me down the corridor, taking a step into the house as she spoke.

I stood and looked up at her. I didn't know her. She had bright orange hair and red lipstick, and a big fluffy coat.

"Where is he?" she repeated, louder, looking at me this time, looking angrily at me and I felt the words on my face like a slap and my cheeks went red. I knew my cheeks were going red.

I didn't say anything because I didn't know what to do. I was distracted by the sharpness on my cheeks and I couldn't think what she might want, all I could think about was the stinging, and the fact I shouldn't be there, and she shouldn't be there.

She made a 'chuh' noise of irritation and pushed my hand out the way, the one that was still holding onto the latch, and she started to walk into the hall. Just as my arm broke free from the latch and fell down by my side, the kitchen door opened at the other end of the hallway. I could hear Uncle Tim yelling something. Then the front door flew back and slammed as a quick sudden breeze flew down the corridor. It nearly knocked the lady over, but she was in the hall by now, trapped in the hall. I was trapped in the hall with her.

All the other noises stopped for a second after the loud crash. I felt a sudden urge to cry.

Uncle Tim was in the corridor, looking confused, blinking at the woman.

"Can I help you?" he said. I didn't know if it was a cross voice or not.

She said, quietly, "Where is he?"
She was looking at the floor.

"Rose! Rose, can you come here a sec?" Uncle Tim called back in the direction of the kitchen, to Mum.

"What are you doing here, eh mate? What are you doing downstairs? Let's get you back up to bed, shall we?"

He put an arm down, around me, and he sounded like he was talking to me, but he didn't look at me, he was looking at her. Then he kept his arm around me though he didn't actually move anywhere until he heard mum come out of the kitchen and rush towards the lady with the bright orange hair.

Uncle Tim guided me upstairs then, and I could hear mum talking to the lady, and she sounded agitated and she had lost the way she was before. She sounded stressed. And then the other man, with the booming voice, was joining in and talking loudly and I heard him say the f word, at least once. You shouldn't say the f word.

And then both mum and the man were telling someone to get out.

The door slammed hard again, but this time it was on purpose.

And then in my bedroom Uncle Tim explained that I was definitely not to go downstairs on any account or under any circumstances, whatsoever. Seriously.

9:30 pm

I wasn't going to go downstairs but I needed to go out to the bathroom. I couldn't sleep, and I needed a wee so badly it felt like a hot splinter in my tummy. I stood up and I felt like I had to bend over a bit and squash my legs together because it hurt, and I was close to having an accident.

As I went to the bathroom I could hear mummy talking to Uncle Tim, in the downstairs hallway again. Uncle Tim sounded more serious than usual, but his voice was a little bit sloppy and he was saying something about someone being married, "for God's sake," and then Mum was shushing him and saying not for much longer, no he doesn't and it's not like that and never, didn't and lots of other 'no' words.

Then Uncle Tim burst out with: "He's got kids, for crying out loud! Why didn't you tell me, sis? What on earth are you playing at?"

And then I rushed to the bathroom because I really knew I shouldn't be listening. And I really needed to wee.

9:49 pm

My film had finished ages ago and I thought I could hear someone coming quietly up the stairs, but I wasn't sure if it was just my imagination. I squeezed my eyes shut in case Mum was checking on me and I listened as carefully as I could. There was a sound like someone hopping one or two steps at a time, lightly, and a sniff, and then I heard the door to Mum's room pushed open as the wood scraped along the thick carpet and made the sound it makes, like paper ripping. And then it was all quiet again, so I opened my eyes, thinking Mum had popped into her room for some reason - and then there in front of me, by the side of my bed, was the lady with the bright orange hair.

The black make-up around her eyes had smudged and run a little bit onto her cheeks. It was worse on one side, and she had clumps of very long, thick eyelashes stuck together so that her left eye looked a little like a squashed insect. Her lipstick had rubbed off in the middle, so it was red on the edge, but pink in the middle, with thin red lines making stripes on her bottom lip.

She sniffed again. For some reason I felt weird, but not scared.

"What's the matter?" I said.
"What's not the matter?"
I didn't know what to say to that.

"Budge over," she said, pushing her knee onto my bedding, to indicate she wanted to sit on my bed, I supposed.

"You're not meant to be up here," I stated.

"No," she said, sitting down. "There's a lot of stuff we aren't meant to do. But I guess the rule book has gone out the window."

A perfectly formed tear was rolling down the side of her nose. It seemed to get bigger as it travelled down until it pooled off her top lip. She left it there, and I wondered if she could feel it at all, and I wanted her to brush it away, but she didn't. When she spoke, it splintered into tiny drops, and some of them fell into her mouth, and others stayed on her lips. I imagined what it tasted like.

"What's your name, kid?" she asked, leaning back onto the bed, with one arm outstretched behind her. She looked like she should be relaxed but wasn't; like she was pretending to be relaxed.

"I'm not allowed to tell people that," I said.

I was a bit scared not to answer her but also proud to have remembered not to tell strangers what I was called.

She snorted.

"That must make things tricky!" she said, "How do you ever introduce yourself? What do they call you in school?"

I didn't understand what she meant. She laughed to herself.

"Never mind," she said.

The weight of her arm and her hip squashed against me and felt like a little mound of cushions, which was pleasant. And she asked me why I was upstairs and about the film I watched and about my dinosaur and if I liked living with my mum, and after a while she seemed to relax a bit and I almost forgot that she wasn't supposed to be there. She was nice. And she stopped crying.

10:04 pm

"Get me a drink, kid?" she said, "A proper drink? A *grown-up* drink."

"Do you mean wine?" I asked. I could feel my eyes hurting and then realised I was staring, and I wasn't blinking.

"That'll do," she said.

I knew mummy would be incredibly cross if she knew the lady was in my room and then if I went downstairs that would be even worse. But the lady still looked just a little bit sad and her make-up was still scribbly, and, in a way, I didn't want her to leave me. She was sat on my bed and it made my feet warm and also it didn't matter that I couldn't sleep anymore because she was just sat there so I wasn't on my own. She grabbed my fingers. Her hand was surprisingly cold and small.

"Please," she said.

I whispered out of bed again and out into the corridor. As I went through the door I heard her say "Good boy," very quietly, and I smiled to myself, and I felt brave.

10:08 pm

Everyone had gone into the lounge and they were playing different music. It was fast and modern. It didn't sound like Mum's music at all. Someone's coat had fallen off the coat pegs in the hall and there was a small patch of a dark drink on the black and white tiles, like coffee maybe. I could hear loud voices but not so much laughter anymore.

I kept my head down and went as quickly as I could into the kitchen. The double doors into the garden were open, slightly. A cool breeze poured into the room like a stream, and the papers on the sideboard flickered.

There were a few plates and lots of glasses on the side, a couple of empty wine bottles and a giant beer bottle. I pulled a green plastic tumbler out of the dishwasher, which was beeping quietly, so I knew it was finished. There was a blue glass bottle and I poured some of the clear liquid into the tumbler. Then a big splash more. I grabbed a half-eaten bowl of peanuts and put it in the crook of my left arm. I walked back towards the hallway, quickly, when I spotted a man, a stranger. He was just coming out of the living room. He saw me, and shut the door behind himself. He put one finger to his mouth. Sshhh.

"Midnight feast, eh?" he said in an exaggerated whisper.

He had a big head, and it was wobbling slightly. His mouth was slightly purple. I didn't like it. His shirt was unbuttoned a little bit and out the top poked some dark grey hair. Wire. His chin was slightly wet.

I didn't say anything. I walked past him quickly and up the stairs, trying not to spill the drink or the peanuts. I didn't want to look at him.

"Sorry about before!" he whispered, close to my face, as I squeezed past him in the corridor and he felt too warm, the wrong temperature.

10:12 pm

The lady with the bright orange hair took a big swig of the drink then snorted loudly, and coughed a high little cough, like a funny bird.

"Bloody hell, what is this? Vodka?" her voice was a bit too loud, "I thought you were getting me white wine!" she cried.

I was worried someone might hear.

"Sorry! I don't know! I didn't know!" I said, and I could hear my voice wailing a little bit like I was younger.

"Hey kid, it's OK You just gave me a shock!" she smiled at me, with a wonky mouth.

While I had been gone, she had done something to her face and make-up. Her left eye didn't look so bad anymore and she had red lips again. She looked very glamorous, like she should be on TV. I told her so, and she raised her plastic tumbler up in the air like people do when they say cheers.

She was asking me more questions about my mum. And she was asking me about my dad. So, I spoke to her, even told her the bits I hadn't told my friends, or my grandma, even the feelings I hadn't told my Mum, because Mum had never asked me. And she didn't seem shocked or surprised, and I felt like she understood, so I told her more and more until I had told her it all, and there was nothing left.

Then we both sat in silence for a few seconds.

She swigged her drink.

"Men are pigs," she said, "present company excepted."

And we sat in silence for a few seconds more.

"Women are pigs sometimes, though, aren't they?" I said. I felt brave to say the words but wanted to hear what she thought.

"He's incredibly selfish though," she said, "in a way that I don't think women are. I don't think any mother would do what he's done; I don't think I'd ever do what he's done."

"What has he done?" I asked.

"Run off with your mum," she stated. She looked me in the eyes. Hard. I felt ashamed.

"Sorry," I said.

"Me too," she said, softly, and she reached over to my hand again. And this time it felt warm.

She smiled, and she tipped the tumbler on its side to show me. It was empty.

"So. It's getting late," she stated. "I think I'd better go."

"Aren't you going to speak to them?" I asked.

I didn't want her to leave, though I had a feeling it might cause trouble if she spoke to mum, or Uncle Tim, or the man, so I was hoping she would say no.

"No. Suddenly doesn't seem like one of my better ideas," she said, pushing herself up off the bed and rearranging her skirt and her big furry coat.

"Well, nice to meet you," she said, sticking her hand out for me to shake.

I shook it, firmly, because that's what you do.

"How are you going to get out?" I asked her.

"Tell your mum she needs to start locking the back door," she said.

She put the tumbler on my bedside cabinet and moved towards the bedroom door, quietly, quickly. I looked up at her and stared hard at all the bits of her, in case I didn't get to see her again. I wanted to be able to remember, with her fluffy coat and her tight shiny skirt, red lips, orange hair.

"I hope things work out, you know, with your husband."

I was trying to be grown up, but I sounded awkward.

She smiled, softly, and looked a bit surprised, raising her black eyebrows slightly.

"Oh, he's not my husband, silly. He's my dad."

And then she left.

Petrichor

She slept, and as she did, I watched her.

Her complexion was perfect. The colour around her eyes, half a shade, perhaps a quarter of a shade darker than the rest of her face. The rest of her skin light, warm. She was illuminated from within.

At times like this, I was back there, back at the beginning. I was dropped from a height, straight in. Plunged deep into the water, over my head - and it was all consuming. It was all around me. This feeling, this terrifying, wonderful feeling. It came on again sometimes with a vengeance, just from the sight of her. Watching her breathe.

I loved her.

She stirred, rolled her head back into the pillow, rubbed one arm, and then a hand, across her face. A little mole. She opened her eyes a fraction and yawned.

"Hey, sleepy head," I said.

She jumped.

"I didn't know you were there," she replied. Suddenly alert.

I chuckled. She gave a small smile.

"I brought you some tea," I said, "it's time to get up. Big day today," and I stroked her hair away from her face, tucked it behind her ear.

I left the room, went downstairs to lay the table, make some toast.

The feeling lingered on my body. It wasn't something I wanted or expected. But it had changed my life. Before I met her, I felt like a fraud, an imposter. I used to wake up thinking, hoping, that any day now I'd know what I was doing. Any day now I'd wake up and be a fully-fledged adult. But when? It was exhausting.

And then it happened. Just when I thought it was almost too late. I met her, and something shifted. I was a grown up. I was secure. This was how things were meant to be.

And now, she came downstairs, dressed all in black. Skinny jeans and a loose t-shirt. She had scraped her hair back into a messy bun. No make-up. Demure.

"Your phone's been buzzing," I stated, as I put down a plate in front of her.

She picked her mobile up.

"Messages from my mum," she said, "asking about today, I guess."

She automatically started on the toast.

I smiled and nodded, though I knew they weren't just from her mum. There were at least two messages from other people. One, from a number I didn't even know.

"There's nothing to worry about," I said, softly, "it'll be ok. And I'll drop you to hers straight after, like we said, OK?"

She looked at me tentatively and nodded, slightly.

"Thank you."

She bit into the toast. I watched her. Crumbs and a piece of the crust fell down, specks, tiny leaves.

"We need to go in ten," I said, and touched her gently across her shoulders.

In the car, we sat in comfortable silence. It was raining slightly, drizzle, and the windscreen wipers creaked across the glass, rhythmically. It was warm; the car steamed up. I smiled gently to myself as she sat beside me: worried, I knew, but strong. She had a solid core that was indomitable. It was both her strength, and her failing.

"I haven't forgotten it's your birthday," I said after a while. I couldn't help myself. I'd told myself not to mention it until the appointment was over.

"I know you haven't," she said quietly, "but we said we wouldn't make a big thing about it. We said we'd focus on the appointment. Let's leave it,"

"I know, I know. It's just a lot of stuff at once. So much going on today. I didn't want it to get completely lost," I said, and paused, "Good stuff, though, of course," I added.

"Good stuff," she said, quietly.

She stared out the window, away from me. She was away.

"I got you a present anyway," I stated.

She turned her head towards me, slowly.

"Did you? We said you wouldn't do that. We need to save money. I can't get a job now. We need the money," she spoke with a flat tone; she was bothered, but always steady these days, calm.

"Hey, I didn't say I'd got you a Mercedes, or a diamond ring!"

She flinched, slightly.

"I just wanted to get you a little something. I can never repay you for what you've done for me," I stated.

She nodded. Went back to looking straight ahead, through the cloudy windscreen.

"Thanks," she said.

"We owe each other now," I added, an aside. She nodded again.

"So, do you know what to expect?" I asked, "With the scan?"

"I think so," she said, "Jen told me about it,"

I gave a little snort, I couldn't help it. Jen. I had hoped she wasn't still talking to her. I thought they'd grown apart; she hadn't mentioned her recently, and I'd been glad.

The drizzle turned to rain and the wipers started to glide peacefully across the screen - though a small patch of light was trying to break through the clouds, trying hard to break through the mist.

"How long will you be in there?" I asked, "I could wait at the car park."

"Oh, I don't know. Because it's the first one, I think they probably weigh you, or whatever. Ask you questions and things."

"You don't have to tell them anything you don't want to, sweetheart," I said, softly, "it's your body. It's your baby."

"I know," she said.

We drove along steadily through the traffic. In spite of the rain, the sun was strong and brutal.

"I'm sorry you'll be on your own," I said, "You know I can't come: I would, if I could," I said, in a rush.

We turned into the hospital car park. I found a space at the back, under a tree, tucked away. I turned off the engine. The rain had stopped and the sun had broken through. The light splintered out of the clouds in shards. We sat together comfortably. We both knew we were waiting until the clock said five to, before she would go. Three minutes left. Just three minutes.

Her phone vibrated.

"I love you," I said. I turned to face her, took her right hand in mine, "remember that. I will always look after you. I will always be there for you," my voice broke slightly. I didn't know why.

She looked down at our hands, a tangle of fingers. She stroked the back of my hand with her thumb.

"I love you, too," she said, but her voice was a murmur, a mirror.

"I'll wait here, then after we can get a coffee, you can tell me all about it. Then I'll take you to your mum like I said. Then this evening, later on, I'll pick you back up - the usual place - and we'll get some food."

She didn't nod this time. Her thumb was still rubbing me, a little too fast; it was starting to go through me, friction. I put my left hand on top; held her thumb securely, stopped the stroking. Held our hands together steadily, warmly. Tight. Together.

At five to, she tugged her hands away, and I let her. She opened the car door. I could hear her mobile buzz. The warm smell of summer rain burst into the car, heavy and unexpected.

"So, dinner, OK?" I said, leaning out of the car, across her vacant seat.

"After all, it's not every day you turn sixteen."

She didn't turn back, started lifting the phone from her pocket when she was just two steps away, before the door had even swung shut. She was probably irritated by her mother, her constant messaging: so needy. I smiled to myself, found myself gently shaking my head, though it wasn't funny. It was a problem.

I watched her walk away, her slim legs, heavy boots. She was slight, quick on her feet, struggling a little with her bag. She was walking fast, off balance, clutching her phone, still.

As I pulled the car away slowly, she rounded the corner to the front of the hospital, and she was safely at the entrance. I crept along, to capture a last glimpse of her as she walked the small flight of stairs; just as I drove past, she reached the top step. She reached the top step and an older male came forward, put one arm around her, bustling her in. He resumed his place at the top of the stairs, standing square on, looking out, eyes searching. And there beside her, reaching forward with both arms, was her mother. Crying; they both seemed to be crying.

I could feel the blood in my veins rising up suddenly, increasing, swelling in my body.

She dropped her bag to the floor and it settled against her leg like an animal, like a guard dog. She bundled herself into her mother's arms.

Instinctively, I pressed the button to open the car window, and the unexpected noise of the hospital burst in, there was a crowd, a murmuration of nurses and patients and visitors. My desperation mingled with their chatter.

I was ready to call out, to reach for her, but the smell of the warm rain settled in my nose and on my tongue, filling my mouth, clogging my words as I drove away.

(Not) Prone to Winking

24th April

She called me from the ladies' toilets. Her voice was fractured, rasping.

"God, I need a cigarette."

"What you need," I countered, "Is a good night's sleep."

"And a glass of Pinot," she said.

"Everyone needs a glass of Pinot," I stated. "Always."

"And it might help the sleep, right? Can you meet tonight? This evening, after work?"

There was a slight pause.

"I'm there," I said, "see you at The Fountain at 6."

(Now. What you need to know, ladies and gentlemen, is that Matthew will try to control this story. Control it, like he does everything else.

But we won't let him. Will we? No.)

I might have somewhere else to be, or more likely, be struck by that familiar feeling of pure dread, at the thought of going out. You know how it is. But when she told me she was sick of drinking alone, sick of crying alone, being alone, whatever, I was there. When she wanted to talk, I would listen.

I was a good friend to her.

(Really? Were you?)

The afternoon passed slowly. I kept my head down. At one stage, Ben came via my desk and stood just a little too close, asked how I was. Nosey git. I smiled and joked, tried to get him to move away. I gave him nothing. Not even a sliver. A splinter.

5:30, and I packed up, promptly. Made no eye contact as I left and tried not to make it obvious I was rushing. I made it outside without speaking to a soul, out into the street where the fresh, damp air hit me with some force, filling my nose, my mouth. It was a heady relief, after my day at work, sedentary and warm.

I walked the few hundred metres to the pub.

The air in the bar, as I pushed the door open, smelt sweet, heavy, stale. Soporific. A contrast to the street. The jarring of the two was disorientating. I felt that familiar excitement I experienced, at the thought of seeing her. Ridiculous, juvenile, but joyous.

I went straight to the bar and ordered a bottle of red wine, two glasses, then looked around for a suitable table.

By the time she arrived, I had drunk two thirds of my first glass.

(As usual.)

She sat down, two carrier bags fell to her feet and moulded against her ankles and shins, as she started to shrug off her jacket. She looked harassed; strands of her hair had fallen down, her lipstick reduced to a faint line around the edge of her lips; a slight greasy crease of eye-shadow sat on her eyelids. Nothing much more than a rumour of a made-up face, from the morning, remained.

But she still managed to look beautiful.

(Now that, I can believe…)

"So," I began, picking up the bottle, "what gives?"

('What gives?' Really? I've never heard you say that in your life, Matthew. More likely it was: 'Alright?')

"I won't bore you with the details," she muttered, "Just someone being a dick at work. And I'm over-tired. Over my job too. Obviously."

"You seemed pretty keen to talk about it earlier. Come on. Spill," I said, and raised an eyebrow.

"Hmm. Well. OK."

She gave a half-hearted lift of her glass to me, a 'cheers', and took a big slug.

"I was in a meeting, and someone snapped at me. Someone more senior; much more senior. And I wasn't ready for it and I was in a fragile mood and I just started crying. Quietly. But crying. It must have been visible: my nose would be red - it's always red when I cry – and I actually had this stream of tears running down my face, alongside my nose. And I couldn't stop them."

"Right. Shit. What did you do?"

"I stayed in the room. I mean, it was embarrassing. But if nothing else it showed me I was hanging on. That's what I kept thinking. Just about hanging on. I wasn't going to let those bastards feel sorry for me. So, I fronted it out. I stayed. They might be uncomfortable, but screw them. I was there. I was present."

The last few words were cracked.

(Jeez, Matthew. There is no way I was that dramatic. Or pretentious.)

"Wow," I said, and then, quickly, "Good for you. Sod them."

She was leaning forward, clutching her glass stem with both hands. The right sleeve of her cream blouse had fallen into a tiny puddle of wine, now blooming pink in a small oasis on her arm. I could smell her Chanel.

"Why am I like this?" she said, quietly, "I've had enough, mate."

(I do not say 'mate'.)

I gave what I hoped was a comforting smile.

"Do you think it's Paul?" she said, "It's been three months now. It seems almost like a lifetime ago, to be honest. But when I think back on it…"

She shuddered.

I did not want to reflect on Paul, not again. That bastard had taken up more of my time and energy than I cared to calculate. This was a pot-hole I did not want to fall into. This was a cavern I did not want to enter.

(This is one thing we can both agree on.)

There was an opaque pause. I looked at my drink. She looked at me, and then at the table.

"Ok," she said, "So what are we drinking to? We need something positive to toast. Any good football results lately? Come on… You've got to give me something!"

I laughed, and we moved on, we chattered an inane chatter and I got to hear some gossip. The kind of gossip you don't get in my line of work, my kind of office. It was a light conversation but interspersed within in it, I tried to show her I cared, that I was there for her. That every single time she fell, she could fall at my feet, and if she thought she would fall to the ground, I would catch her, like this.

(And there we have it. Matthew the hero. The white knight. Looking for someone to save.

Looking for a victim.)

30th May

She was late. I was sat at a table in the Arts Centre, pretending to immerse myself in some sort of South American music. She was late, usually late these days.

(Ok, that's true. But I had my reasons. He's not giving you the back-story. He's not giving you my story.)

I picked at a small dish of olives on the table. I do not like olives. She was worth the wait, yes. But it was still irritating.

My phone vibrated. I picked it up, and on the screen, I could see a text from her: 'on way'.

(It had a smiley face and a kiss. I'm sure it had a smiley face and a kiss.)

I was vaguely irritated. But glad, relieved. That familiar feeling was falling back over me again, further and further, as natural as gravity, and as heavy. I was excited, jittery to see her, always. But I felt scared, a little out of control, off centre. I couldn't curtail the feelings. Even if she took me for granted, just a little. Even though I could see she wasn't perfect. I was drawn to her. She had the upper hand on me.

(I told you. He even said it himself. The very word. Control.)

I called my mum, picked at the olives, drained a bottled beer. Eventually, she came.

"Hey," I said, half standing, when I saw her. I could feel my face flush.

"Sorry, sorry, sorry," she rushed at me, leant in for a cheek kiss, "Nice shirt!" she said, playfully into my ear, tugging at it as she did so.

Was she flirting?

(Err, no.)

She put her handbag down on the table, with a clumsy, quick clatter. I looked at her, quizzically.

"Don't ask," she said, laughing, "I really am sorry. I definitely owe you a drink," she said.

"Just a drink?" I said, teasing.

"OK You're right. I deserve that. Dinner's on me," she smiled.

We sat that night and talked intensely for hours. She told me about Davy, a man she had met at a private viewing of an art exhibition.

"Since when do you go to private viewings of art exhibitions?" I laughed.

She giggled, wrinkled her nose.

"Work," was her only reply.

"I'm not sure they'd suit you," I said.

(Who are you to decide that, Matthew? Stop trying to pigeon hole me.)

He was younger than her. Gorgeous, apparently. Not *the* artist, but *an* artist, nonetheless. Rolled his jeans up over his ankles, had a tattoo on his hand. That sort of thing.

(Way to be dismissive and condescending, 'mate'.)

She was intrigued by him, animated, as she told me the tale of how they met, and the few dates since, which had varied between intense, passionate, heady evenings together to occasions where he had barely spoken to her all evening.

I didn't like it. I didn't like the way she was sparkling at the thought of him. And I didn't like the way she described him, their relationship. He was dangling her. Taking advantage. It was pretty clear he was abusing the fact she was so keen.

She had her phone on the table. Kept glancing at it. She picked it up a few times, to check the screen, even though there were clearly no messages there.

She saw me looking.

"Sorry," she said, "I know it's crap of me. It's just I haven't heard from him today and I thought he'd text. Pathetic, aren't I?"

She gave a little chuckle, opened her bag to retrieve a lipstick and started dabbing on, at the table. It was bright, intoxicating. It hit against the white of her skin and the mid-brown of her hair, giving me a sudden jolt again.

She was Cadmium Red, she was Carmine, Crimson, Burnt Sienna.

(Oh, God.)

I smiled at her, gently, tried to quell my feelings, to make sure it wasn't obvious.

"You should wear that more often," I said, "It suits you."

Glancing down at her phone again, she smiled back, eyes flitting between me and it; me and him. And I realised that under the paint, the thick, peeling paint, perhaps there was a version of her that was ready to be with me. Almost ready to be with me.

(I don't know where you got that from, Matthew. That was a rather worrying take on the whole evening. Over thinking, much?)

26th June

It was finished with Davy. She didn't seem that upset in the end. Just annoyed with herself, for letting it limp on for so long, it seemed. She was bitter, just a little, but on a high. Looking for a fresh start. She'd got a new haircut, it bounced just under her chin, a good three inches shorter than it had been the last time we'd met.

"I'm moving on," she said, "I'm growing. I won't be making a stupid mistake like that again."

But a clean sweep is just a memory of a dirty past.

We chattered away, comfortably. She didn't ask about me.

(I didn't have to. If you recall, you spent the first twenty minutes of that meeting regaling me with the ins and outs of the row you'd had with your brother that weekend.)

We'd been sat for around 40 minutes when a friend of hers came over, I didn't recognise her, and she didn't introduce me.

(I couldn't remember her name, actually.)

When the woman - whoever she was - mentioned she had just gotten divorced I made my excuses and went to the bathroom. I took my time, paid for the coffees on my way back, and by the time I reached the table again she had left.

"She just invited me to a party. Her sister's 50th. I hardly know the woman!"

Her smile was broad and genuine: she was pleased, flattered.

"That's nice," I said. Unsure what else I could contribute: felt strangely thrown off by this information.

"It's a garden party. A big affair, apparently. I guess she wants to make sure there's no shortage of guests! Seems a bit early in the summer to be risking an open-air event... I hope there's a marquee," she said, and paused, a little pinch forming between her eyebrows, "What should I wear?"

"So, you're going then;" I said, "not like you to enjoy a room full of strangers."

(You see how he is? Always trying to tell me what I do and don't like.)

"A garden full of strangers is a completely different thing," she smirked, "Well, apparently there will be simply dozens of eligible men there. And champagne. You know I could never say no to that."

"The men?" I asked, "Or the champagne?"

She winked.

My heart contracted a little.

(It is highly unlikely that I winked. I am not prone to winking.)

9th July

I arrived second, for once. I could see she had been crying; her nose was pink, shiny. In front of her she had an unopened bottle of prosecco, in an ice bucket.

"Hey," she said, as I approached. Quickly, she began shoving crumbled tissues into her bag.

I bent down to kiss her cheek. She smelt of cigarettes.

"Hi... Ok?" I asked.

"I got some fizz!" she said, without answering, "To celebrate your promotion!"

A faint smile, that didn't reach her eyes.

"What's the matter?" I said, as I sat down.

Immediately, she started to cry. She dropped her head, cocooned herself into herself, her knees crossed tightly and her arms hugging her body. I couldn't see her face, but her shoulders shuddered: she was sobbing.

(Yes, Ok, I did do that. I hope he tells you why.)

She told me a story, a long tale, a cornucopia of issues involving a man she had met – I wasn't sure where.

(This was not the main focus of what I said; why start with that?)

And she talked about work, of course, and her boss, and one of her friends, or a colleague, who was ill, apparently. It was a ball of string, a red thread flowing from one thing to another, weaving a pattern of connections and pity that wasn't actually there. Joining dots together, in a configuration that never really existed.

(You utter bastard, Matthew.)

I watched her that evening, as she spoke, and there were flashes of her old self, of my old feeling. But it was a broken flashlight. There were snippets, quick blasts. Yet it was inconsistent. It was waning.

I started to think I'd had enough.

(A 'good friend', were we?)

26th July

I met her from work, a Friday night. She had already been out a little while, something about a late work lunch and no need to go back to the office.

(It was a funeral. For a colleague. A wake.)

Her eyes sparkled. She was in a sentimental mood, part emotional, part playful. Sometimes verging tears, but weird, happy tears, meaning-of-life tears. Up and down.

(Yes. I'd been to a funeral.)

Her make-up was smudged a little around her left eye, and her breath smelt of stale lager. I was tired of it by then, I realised. She was ranting on a little, about missed opportunities and growing up, and getting old.

(A funeral.)

I suddenly realised she was hinting. She was leaning into me, across the table. Her two arms crossed over, elbows on the table, trying to look demure, I guessed, but coquettish. I could see her right knee, poking up, her shin smooth and shiny, disappearing behind the round table. She was wearing red nail varnish, crimson, and touched her cheek with the index finger on her left hand.

(This is not how it was. This is not what happened.)

"I feel good, you know, in a weird way, in spite of it all," she was saying, "Like I have moved into a different phase. Moved on. Grown up a bit."

She was slurring, very slightly.

(I was not.)

"I've applied for that job, you know. I might not get it, but it's a first step, right? And I feel better about myself. It's like I've suddenly realised: I can do it. I'm a grown up. And I don't need these… *boys*… hanging around me, distracting me, holding me back."

She emphasised the word 'boys', and as she did so, she leant even further in, and made eye contact with me. Hard.

(I did not.)

And that was the moment. I sat back, quickly. Dropped my hands into my lap. She stayed where she was. We both sat in silence a moment. I grabbed my phone from my pocket, pretended to look at the time.

"God, sorry, I have to go. Is that the time? I should have said, I'm meeting mum," I blurted. I didn't even bother to make it realistic.

I downed most of the rest of my pint.

"Sorry, I feel bad, sorry, but I do have to go; will you be OK?"

And as I was saying it, I was starting to stand, already starting to stand. I didn't care really, wasn't bothered if

she knew. I needed to get away from her. She was a leech, she was a parasite, she was Cochineal. And I was over it.
  I realised I didn't want her any more.
  (I realised he never was my friend.)

Boulder

I think it may have shocked me even more than it did him.

It happened very quickly, a reflex. Joe said something, I don't remember what exactly, and I found myself launching a punch at his face – clumsy, yet surprisingly impactful. I can still see it clearly. My fist, only half clenched, powering swiftly into his face. My ring scraping his cheek bone and then creating a sharp and extraordinary slice, close to his left eye. The blood sprayed a few tiny droplets onto his white shirt. Irregular but neat.

The footprints of a broken bird.

The look on his face was unlike any expression I had ever observed on him before. I had seen him angry sometimes - disappointed often. But not like this. His mouth was apart, his eyebrows lifted. It was disbelief, but behind it, somewhere, was the hint of a smirk.

We stood still together for a while, in silence. Then I picked up my wine glass again and took a large slug.

"So that's it, is it?" he said, after a while, shaking his head slightly, with one hand to his face.

"What do you mean?" I replied, quietly.

"You carve a chunk out of me and don't even comment on it? For God's sake, aren't you even going to apologise? Don't you care? What the hell's the matter with you?"

He was getting angry now, eyes flitting around the room, from side to side.

I took a step back. Leant against the work top, cradling my wine. Then I started to shake, shake so deeply inside me, so quickly, that I was vibrating. I was pulsating.

"I'm sorry."

"You're sorry," he said, flatly. He took his hand from his face and looked at the blood. "You're sorry."

His eye had started to puff up, slightly.

"You're getting worse. You need help. I'm telling you, you need to sort yourself out. I can't take your behaviour anymore; this has been going on too long. I'm so... ashamed... that I put up with you. I mean it. Sort it out, or get out," he was speaking quickly, staccato. "I should report you. This is assault."

I looked down into my wine glass; it was almost empty but the last few dregs were throbbing as I shook.

I pictured the sea, rings of water circling the space where a boulder had been dropped in. A stone.

"I know," I said. "I'm sorry."

He seized a tea towel and started dabbing at the blood on his shirt, his face, and stared at me as he did so, and then, all of a sudden, he bolted out the room.

I finished my glass of wine. Poured another.

****

Sometimes I felt like I had no control over anything. My emotions, my money, my life. I could be sat on a bus and suddenly feel the urge to cry. I could walk into a shop and suddenly feel the urge to buy a mound of junk food. I could be queuing in the bank, the post office, the supermarket and suddenly feel the urge to leave. I didn't even know how I felt; how to describe the mood, the state of mind. I couldn't tell you if I was happy or sad.

I did know I was scared. I did know that.

Over two years I had seen a deterioration in body and health that had matched my mental state. I tried to hide it, with black and baggy clothes, extra make-up. I was fooling no one. My face was puffed, a lack of sleep, and wine, no doubt. My skin had even changed shade. I was ashamed of my arms – once toned, tanned and attractive; I never had them on display anymore. My torso had ballooned into bloated mounds and rolls. I knew it disgusted Joe. I didn't blame him.

And my behaviour was erratic. Often, Joe had sat with me, rational, calm, while I screamed or cried or felt like I would snap: a thread, a string. It must have been exhausting just to be around me.

So, no, I had never lost control so outwardly and obviously before.

But I had been out of control for a very long time.

****

The next day, Joe had a bruise and a small scab. His eye was swollen, just a little. He was making tea in the kitchen, and strangely seemed to be hobbling, as if stiff or injured. I couldn't think what I'd done to make him move like that. He seemed tired; old.

I scratched in my mind for a memory, another incident, but nothing came up. Except the punch, of course. I watched him moving around the room, from one unit to another, from one side to another.

Then he put both hands down on the counter, either side of his tea, to steady himself. He seemed weary. He breathed in and out deeply, staring down into the mug, and then steadily turned to face me.

"I want you to hand yourself in."

I snorted. I couldn't help it. I was so taken aback. I felt both my hands whip up to my face, my mouth, trying to stop the noise from escaping. But it was too late.

He closed his eyes and breathed in and out. Opened them again.

"I want you to go to the Police station and hand yourself in. I want you to tell them what you did to me. I need you to take some responsibility for the way you've been acting. I need you to show me you are sorry, and I want you to get help. They'll make sure you get help,"

"Joe..." I began, falteringly.

"No. Listen. If you love me, and you are sorry, this is what you will do,"

I pulled the sleeves of my top further down, tucked the cuffs into the palms of my hand, my fingers. He looked down at my hands, clasped as they were into half-fists.

"But Joe," I said, my voice cracked, vibrating, buzzing almost, "I can get help without going to the Police. And I don't think they'll care. It was only one punch."

As soon as I said it, I regretted it. My hands were up at my mouth again, my stupid mouth, too slow, too late; my hands, my stupid hands.

There was a heavy pause.

"I'm asking you to do this," Joe stated, steadily, "and if you don't do it, within the next 24 hours, I want you out."

"But where will I go? How can I pay for anything? Where do you expect me to go to?"

I could feel the desperation flickering inside me. He meant it. I knew it. And I would be utterly lost without him. I had nothing, nothing left.

"You should have thought of that before," his teeth were gritted, "This is your fault. You did this. This!"

He pointed at his face, seemed to remember the pain, and tentatively prodded and then stroked his wound.

****

The one and only friendship I had managed to maintain was with Caitlin. She is energetic, strong, and, thankfully, non-judgemental. I hadn't told her how I was feeling, but to some extent she probably knew. She must have seen the change in me.

Joe didn't like her, talked about her as a 'bad influence' as if we are teenage girls. He frowned when I mentioned her name, a little pinch between his eyebrows, a stare over my shoulder, not into my face.

I was not a good friend. I did not take part in many heart-to-hearts. I frequently cancelled plans. I didn't even always remember birthdays.

But she was, she was a good friend. She is. Steadfast; a rock.

****

Caitlin sat across from me at her kitchen table. Between us was a plate of cupcakes, some eaten, some untouched; little mounds of crumbs like sand, in between the cases. She was incredulous.

"He wants you to do *what*?"

"Hand myself in," I repeated.

"Jesus Christ," she stated. "It makes it sound like the crime of the century."

"Assault is a serious offence," I ventured.

"Yes. Of course, it is," she replied, eyes as slits, leaning forward, "You were provoked. You must see that."

"He says it's Actual Bodily Harm. He says he probably should have had stitches. I can't even remember what happened, to make me do it. It's strange. It's all like a swamp when I think about it. I do remember his face though, and afterwards, his reaction."

I squeezed the sleeves of my top between my fingers.

"You can't possibly be thinking of doing it?" Caitlin asked.

"I can't remember what happened before. So that means I could do it again, doesn't it? It could be worse? I could do anything. I could really hurt him. Or someone else. I need to do something about it. I can't carry on like this. What am I going to do?"

I burst into tears, sobs, heaving and gulping through my body. My hands – those hands – were shaking as I lifted them up to my face to catch the tears.

"Ok," she said. "We will go. If that's what he wants. We will go," she stated. "We'll tell them the whole thing. Everything."

We locked eyes.

I told you she was a good friend.

****

I went home and went straight upstairs, while Caitlin waited in the car. Joe was out, but I felt the urge to creep and rush through the house, anyway – a stranger's home.

Upstairs, I took a deep breath and sat down. I placed myself at the dressing table and carefully removed all my make-up, scraped my hair back. I took a hard look at the face in the mirror. Impassive, cold, pale, patchy. Marble.

I put on a new set of clothes; didn't worry about hiding the full length of my arms today. Didn't feel the need to grip my fingers in fabric, grip them into little fists again. I was changing my ways.

I ran back downstairs, swift, efficient, grabbed my bag and went out to Caitlin in the car. She looked at me, make-up free, exposed; she saw the reality of my complexion, my face, my expression, and simply nodded.

She started the car and drove us in silence.

At the Police station there was a short queue. The room was grey, and crowded, chilled: I felt my legs shaking, wondered if I could really do this, wondered if I had the grit inside me, the shingle, the stone. Caitlin held my elbow; propelled me forwards each time someone left the line. There was constant noise around us, a strange cacophony, collapsing desperate and emotional tones with the everyday, the mundane. Caitlin stood close to me, the scent of her perfume was in my nose, and her warmth was there. I could hear her breathing, shallow and fast. It struck me that she was nervous, too.

"You can do this," she whispered.

Finally, eventually, it was our turn. The woman at the counter was behind a thick shield of Perspex, and her voice was amplified out to me, on my side, tinny and hollow. She gave a faint and weary smile.

"How can I help you, today?" she asked.

"I'm here to report an assault," I said.

And I lifted up my arms so that the sleeves of my top fell further away, to show her the bruises and fingerprints that covered them. Joe's fingers, Joe's hands, that covered my skin as graffiti - his signature sprayed across me, over and over again; blue, green, brown, and yellow shocks, against the cold alabaster of my body.

The Day I Nearly Drowned

The day I nearly drowned, I was wearing a new swimming costume.

Mum had always given me plain, navy, one-piece suits: sometimes second-hand, I realised now – their thin, elastic threads poking through the sheen of the fabric in barbs.

Grandad must have felt sorry for me; me with my prickly, shiny costume. Me, with legs of sinew, matted hair, overloaded, curling in. Me, trampled by loss and shame. Fear.

So, he bought me a two-piece bikini. Bright red, with little frills. And he said we should go swimming at the local pool.

"Do you good," he stated, "Something normal."

But swimming in a frilly two-piece felt far from normal to me.

We had spent some time together in the shallow end of the 'big pool', its icy water exciting, grey – smashed to smithereens around me by teenage boys balling into the water with confidence, and volume.

After a little while, I was chilled, bored. Grandad was holding the edge, clinging to tiles and chatting to someone I didn't know. The odd word reached me: "Yes, with me now,"; "doing OK"; "a terrible shock to all of us".

My little feet padded towards the bottom of the pool, to keep warm, occupied, afloat, as I clung to the side.

I turned to the ladder beside me and stepped a foot on the bottom rung, thinking of the kiddie's pool, and its warmer, softer sea, where children would plonk into the water, not hurtle.

I managed the ladder with surprising ease and scuttled over to the smaller pool, considering the approach we usually took, with its sloping decline. I thought better of this, wondered why we never took the ladder at the other end. Like the ladder I had managed myself, alone, so confidently.

I started to step myself in; after three steps, I detached from the bars of the ladder, to tread the bottom of the pool on tiptoe. But it was not there. Just a wall of water, pressure against my legs as I waved them in desperation to find ballast.

I was slipping, falling underneath.

Up and then under, up and then under for longer and I opened my eyes into the liquid, looking for a way out. Children's feet and adult's hands were just out of reach, as chum, around me. The weight on my chest. Compression.

I caught a glimpse of my own pony tail, floating and knotting ahead.

I was not breathing.

But then I was plucked, bursting out of the pool into the air, the hard air, and I was back on the edge - liquid pouring from nose, eyes, fabric, the red strap of my bikini top pulled down over my shoulder. My hair a net, plastered against my neck. My legs not my legs, a stranger's legs, beneath me.

I was a tangle of limbs, shivering, confused. Around my arms, my body, were knotted someone else's limbs. Intertwined.

"It's OK," a low voice repeated, "It's OK, love. I'm here."

A Pane of Glass Between Them

She stood on the platform, waiting for her mother.

To her left, two teenagers were curled on a bench. A girl sat in - and across - a boy's lap. Every time the girl wriggled, he would rearrange himself so that his arms snapped back into an all-encompassing embrace. They were layer upon layer of limbs; a knotted ball of string. It looked uncomfortable, she thought, as she turned away.

Damn, she was getting old.

The clock on the platform had cracked glass but seemed accurate. The train was due any moment. She took a deep breath and closed her eyes. She tried to use her diaphragm but could feel the breath - tight, stuck. Anticipation had its claws around her neck and it pinched her gullet into a tube, no bigger than a vein.

She never knew what to expect with her mother.

The train filled the station - and she braced herself.

****

"Cup of tea, mum?" she called from the kitchen, with her hand poised to hit the 'on' switch.

Paused and waited; raised her eyes to heaven.

"CUP OF TEA, MUM?" she called, again.

"What? No, no..." Joy muttered.

Joy glanced around the room. It was all different again. Some bizarre, black furniture now occupied the space where the pink armchair had been. She liked that pink armchair. Why had she got rid of it?

"Why have you got rid of the pink armchair?" Joy said to her as she came back into the room. Barefoot, she was. No shoes.

"It needed replacing. Don't you like my new sofas?"

"What do you mean 'needed replacing'? There was nothing wrong with it,' - a short exhale and slight, but perceptible, shake of the head. Twitchy and jittery. A cricket.

"It did mum, it was old. Take a seat, will you?"

"Hah! Old. I'm old. I suppose you'll be replacing me, will you? There was a time when people bought things to last. It's all right for some, eh? Buying new things every year. I would have had it if you said."

"Mum, you're not old. You're 63," she said.

"62," Joy corrected.

She was glancing around the room, trying to get her bearings. Everything was slightly out of kilter. Nothing quite looked right, or the same. But what? She couldn't put her finger on it. It was like one of those games where you look at a tray, then close your eyes, and they take something away. And you guess what it is. Like a game. A trick. They do that to you sometimes.

"You haven't even been here in two years! How do you know what the chair looked like? Anyway, you live three hours away... how would you have got it home if I gave it to you?"

Her voice was rising, a little flush came to her cheeks. (Old.)

"Oh, come on mum, sit down."

Joy sat down on the edge of the sofa, still with her coat on. She placed her handbag next to her and periodically patted it, like a little kitten.

She went into the kitchen again, briefly, then came back with a plate of biscuits.

"Have a cookie, mum," she said, leaning over her and holding out a shiny, square plate.

It struck Joy as strange to have a shiny, square plate.

"No. I'm not mad on these crumbly biscuits. They're a bit salty. I like Garibaldis. Do you like Garibaldis?" she said, looking up at her suspiciously, and her shiny, square plate.

"Nobody likes Garibaldis, mum," she said, with a sort of sigh.

But that didn't even make any sense.

****

The warmth of the wood burner, and the dimmed lighting, made everything easy and cosy. She looked across at her mother and smiled to herself to see mum frowning slightly at the TV, but definitely looking more relaxed. She had finally persuaded her to take off her coat - although she still had one hand on her bag. She smiled.

"You OK, mum? Do you want anything?' Softly, she spoke. She did not want to fracture the mood. It was a fragile thing. Crystal.

Joy looked over and smiled.

"Got any of those biscuits?" she said.

****

Joy woke with a start, as if someone had lifted her torso from the bed then savagely slammed it down. It was that dream again.

She was drenched in sweat; muscles constricted.

Always the same. She was running through town, running down the stairs to the Tube, running holding his little hand, hurrying him up. The same. Laughing, red faced. Running together. Running losing his hand. Looking back. Onto the train. Running and the doors were shutting and then he was shut out and not behind her anymore. Why was he not behind her anymore? Dirty windows, dirty doors. She could not see. She could not see him. And then a piercing scream and the emergency button and then the doors were opened, and he was gone.

Running up and down the platform but he was gone. He was lost.

****

She put a glass teapot on the table. Glass. And no placemat.

"How are you, mum?" she asked, absently, pushing a mug towards Joy.

"I dreamt about him," Joy said.

"Oh, mum."

Her shoulders dropped, and she walked away from the table, back into that other room, the little room she kept disappearing into. She walked in again a few moments later, carrying a carton of long-life milk. Why did she have long-life milk?

"It's only a dream, mum…. So, did you think about what I said? Do you want to go to see the sea?"

"He didn't get on the train." Joy said.

"It would take about 45 minutes or so, but it's quite a nice day, so it would be worth it," she continued.

She sat down and poured herself tea into a mug, then milk. Not enough milk.

"The doors shut, and when they opened he was missing."

"There's this tearoom there. We went once before; you remember. They do those huge Victoria sponges," she said.

She was talking quickly, softly, a little stream of sound. No, steam of sound. Steam, hot air on glass. What was she saying?

"He was gone. Where did he go?" Joy looked up, tears in her eyes. "Why did I lose him?"

"You know this isn't helpful, mum," she said, firmly.

****

The girl in the café placed a three-tiered cake stand on the table between them. It was laden with miniature eclairs, scones. The plates were three different shades of blue and matched the tea-cups already on the table. It looked beautiful.

"Wow," she said, and smiled, leaning right into the table.

Joy gave a slight tilt of the head, a half smile.

"Lovely," she answered. But turned her body, just a fraction, away from the table – away from her.

Joy had crossed her legs to one side and her right leg was swinging up and down, swiftly.

She put one scone, one panna cotta and one éclair on Joy's plate. She passed it over. They sat, and ate.

"I didn't expect us to walk so far. It was great, though. I love the beach; it's been too long… and you're fitter than me!" she wet her index finger and jabbed at the crumbs on her plate.

"It's a wonderful beach." Joy said.

"I know! It is! Maybe you should come back in the summer. We could go on one of those boat trips, or something?"

There was warmth there, in the words. True warmth. Yet Joy stayed silent. A tiny pinch came and went from her forehead, between her eyes.

"I might get a bike," she said, enthusiastically. "I should get a bike. I used to love my bike. Then I took it to Uni and it got nicked. Remember? I could ride here. It's not that far…"

Joy looked up at her and wondered why she was always asking her if she remembered.

"We've had a good day, haven't we mum?"

"I just wish… you know… he was here," Joy said, quietly.

She sat back quickly, dropped both hands to the table.

"No, I'm here, mum. I am," she said.

****

Joy woke up early and came downstairs. She poured herself a glass of water and sat down at the table. It was still littered with things from dinner, the night before: a cruet set; a wine glass; a dirty knife. She noticed a small, dark red stain on a tea-towel.

And then she came in, shuffling stiffly.

"Morning. You're up early!"

Joy played with the edge of the tea-towel between two fingers.

"Is that blood?" Joy asked.

"Is what blood?" she replied, irritated, as she walked to the kitchen.

"Nothing."

She put the tea-towel down.

It was very odd to leave this stuff out on the table. Did she do it on purpose? Maybe she wanted her to see it.

"Someone called my mobile last night. A man telling me that I was owed money because of a loan, twenty years ago it was." Joy said, while she looked at her distorted reflection on the blade of the dirty knife.

"You didn't talk to him? You didn't do anything?" she sounded worried, was standing in the door-frame, staring.

"No. He must think I was born yesterday."

But what she really wanted to know was how he got her number. And why had he picked her? But Joy hesitated to say this aloud, knew it was the sort of thing that would make her cross.

"Did you sleep well?" Joy asked, instead.

"Hhmm," was the only answer.

She was back at the table now, clearing away the blood-splattered cloth and that wine glass. Clearing away the strange things that should never have been there. Why were they there?

"Well, aren't you going to ask me how I slept?" Joy asked.

She stopped what she was doing and paused. She looked into Joy's eyes.

"How did you sleep, mum?"

"You know how I slept," Joy stated.

"Oh, for God's sake!" she snapped, "That's it! I can't stand it! You're always the same... it's always this. Why do you come? I don't get it. This.... Just piss off, mum! Piss off, will you? Piss off for once and... and... stop coming back!"

And she threw the tea towel. She actually threw the tea towel. It clipped the salt-pot as it went and there was a clutter of porcelain and salt crystals and shock alongside it. Joy jumped, but continued to stare at the table. Then they both kept still until the salt-pot stopped rolling and the reverberations settled.

And when it was over, the words hung in the air, a pane of fractured glass, between them.

****

They stood together on the platform. They hadn't spoken since they arrived, had barely spoken since breakfast. Joy had never tolerated swearing, and they had rarely had a truly cross word, despite it all, despite everything.

She wondered if this was it, the final straw, if she could really bring herself to cut her mother out of her life, as she had thought of doing, so often. A little flicker of excitement tremored in her stomach at the thought. She might do it. She could do it. Should she?

What sort of person would that make her?

"Well," Joy said, "one minute to go."

"Yes."

"At least we weren't late; at least we weren't rushing. We didn't run."

"No," she said.

The train was upon them in no time, huge and cold and dirty. Joy had a seat; they had to find Coach C. They walked along the platform quickly, but it wasn't busy, it was all very easy. Joy stepped onto the train and then she passed her little, black suitcase to her.

"So, see you then," she said, and tried to give her a quick, unexpected hug, across the gap, through the gap. It became a sort of confused fumble instead.

"Bye, mum."

Joy didn't answer, didn't look at her, but nodded - and as she did so she saw a slight tremor in her face, no, in her head.

The doors made their distinctive noise and then whispered shut. Through the dirty pane of glass, she saw her mother on the other side, turning away from her, moving away - and then taking two steps, and then hidden behind a man, a man slightly obscuring her. And then she was out of sight.

    She was lost.

Bedtime Story

The scream jerked her body like shrapnel. She flicked her eyes open without lifting her head - important, always, to remain as still as possible. It began as a sharp, piercing wail, which undulated and then rose to a peak. An auditory wince.

Her bedsit was one of a number of small flats and rooms, inside what had once been an Edwardian house. Each was separated from the other by little more than plaster board and MDF; she would not be the only one awoken by the cry. It persisted; paused; persisted again. Horrific.

That damn baby.

A few swift blinks and then 2:02 am washed into focus, meaning just another four hours or so and she would have to wake up again. She could not help but feel anger and resentment - surprisingly keenly, given how exhausted she was.

When she was younger, just a little younger, she was often still out at this time of night, happily tripping through the streets, with little thought or care for how much sleep she would gain or lose. Hours on the clock meant nothing; hours in bed could be caught at any time. And now there it was, a great wall of sleep deprivation and fatigue, like a tsunami, trailing behind her and threatening, each day, all day, to engulf her and sweep her away.

How much longer could it go on for? How much longer could she go on for?

And still that baby was crying.

Without coordination, she raised her head from the pillow; it jerked itself square. Then her shoulders, her biceps, her back - until with fingers pushed fast into the sheets and hair plastered to her neck - she finally reached a seated position.

Each swell of the baby's cry made her body flinch.

She grabbed the notepad from her bedside cabinet, knocked the pencil on the floor (naturally) - which made her curse aloud as her hand scrambled around to find it. Reaching the pillow up, she jammed it between her shoulder blades and the bare wall, positioning herself to write today's - tonight's - thoughts. A friend who was a counsellor had suggested this. She made a list of all the things that made her feel anger (or worse still, despair) and then a note of how she could rephrase them, give them a positive twist. Re-think her thoughts. It was to train the brain to think positively; to train her mind not to believe the stream of negativity that flowed through it. This was the plan, at least.

'I'm tired,' she wrote, and, beside this, 'At least I'm alive.'

'I'm getting old,' she wrote, and, beside this, 'At least I'm getting wise.'

'The baby,' she wrote. 'The baby. The baby.'

She threw the notepad across the room - the pencil hit the wall with a satisfying crack, but the book reached only midway before the pages made it flutter to the floor, as a crushed bird.

Sobbing, exhausted, she staggered across the room, and looked down inside the cot.

And there it was still, the crying baby.

****

From: Joe82@JCllanguageschool.com
Sent: Mon 19/03/19 3:59 pm
To: girl@hmail.com
Subject: Hey girl!

Hey girl,

So, haven't heard from you for a couple of days. Just wondering how things are going? Not upset with me about the money, are you? You can't hold that against me … it's sorted now, right? ☺

Things have been pretty quiet at the school. Joao keeps telling me to keep my chin up, because when the summer starts to come around there is bound to be more work in the evenings, and with activities, etc. I guess I'll just have to bide my time and try to be frugal until then.

    I am still planning to come back around July time. I do miss you and can't wait to meet the little one and get to know her. It's an amazing thought really. Blows my tiny mind. I just don't want to come back empty handed, I'd like to save a bit for us - all three of us - and even come back to a job lined up. Who knows? Maybe we could even set up our own language school! You are a natural with the teenagers. (Should come in handy, in future years, eh?)

    Speak soon, love you,

    Joe xxx

****

    The scream hit her face like a cold, grey slap. She flicked her eyes open: 1:38 am There was less and less time between feeds – less and less time to sleep. Somehow, if possible, things seemed to be getting worse.

    Her foot hit the floor before the rest of her body was upright and she lurched out of bed. The cool, laminate floor sent a pulse with each step until she reached the cot-side. She looked down and saw the baby, with its shockingly dark, oily mop of hair - face pink and eyes scrunched tight: a mole. So tiny; so terrifying. She reached into the cot, cooing desperate, soothing sounds as she lifted it to her torso.

    Nobody tells you, before you have a baby, about the agony and the ecstasy; how the rapture and the horror mingle into one; how it is possible to feel such resentment, such responsibility and such sheer adoration at once. But, most of all, an overwhelming sense of fear: that you are doing things wrong, that things will never get better, that you are now responsible for this tiny, miniature, beautiful, noisy bomb that rips your life open and whose own life rests in your hands. Literally. Just when you are at your weakest.

She shuffled to the chair, with the baby snuffling and mewling against her right shoulder, until she was settled enough to lift the front of her t-shirt and allow it to nestle into her breast. Between sucks it continued to let out frustrated little cries until the milk flowed freely and the pair of them could begin to relax.

Reaching forward, she shook the mouse on the table top and brought the computer screen into life.

****

From: Joe82@JCllanguageschool.com
Sent: Thurs 22/03/19 7:57 pm
To: girl@hmail.com
Subject: Re: Hey girl!

Hey,

I spoke to mum today and she was none too happy with me.

Apparently, she bumped into Jenny in the market who told her about our arrangement with the money. I had assumed, obviously foolishly, that we were keeping that to ourselves. You know full well how hard it can be to get work here out of season. There's me doing my damnedest to earn any money I can for us, and there's you blabbing our private lives to your vile step-mother. She even knew about the guitar. Why on earth did you mention it? That thing was an investment and you know it. Like I bloody *want* to go busking on the streets in the middle of March.

Anyway, Joao gave me a sub on the promise that I would cover Marie's shift for the students' shopping trip this weekend - my idea of hell by the way - so I managed to transfer €100 into your account today. Check it.

I hope you are as loose with your tongue about the good news as you are about the bad.

I am trying, you know.

J

****

The scream cut the air like a splinter of glass. 1.39 a.m. Too early for a feed. She slipped a foot out of bed onto the cool floor, stumbled over to the cot, and looked inside. A pink, wrinkled face met her eyes. She picked up the baby and began to rock it. She held it tight and firm to her chest. Still it wailed.

She paced around the small confines of the room. It wailed.

She paced some more.

She pulled the cord on the mobile hanging above the baby's bed. Brahms' lullaby played into the shocked night air. What was wrong with the child? Why couldn't she make it happy? The baby wailed. Still.

After a few more minutes, she rested on the wooden chest that housed her clothes at the foot of her bed and swayed her whole torso back and forth. Eight minutes, ten minutes passed until she jumped back into a standing position when she felt her head jerk to her shoulders in the promise of sleep.

But still.

Recently, she had read an article about how experiencing stress, by proxy, could actually alter the way a baby's brain develops, and about how inconsistency of response from the mother in the first few months - even in the first few weeks - could affect the way children relate to all adults in later life. Moreover, apparently the levels of stress a mother experiences during pregnancy, and the chemical and hormonal changes these cause, could even have a negative impact upon the way a baby's brain develops - in the womb. The womb!

More guilt. Leading to more stress.

She squashed the emotions, the feelings, the tiredness into a little, hard ball in the pit of her stomach. Don't feel it; please don't feel the pain.

She kissed the baby's forehead and it smelt of warmth and pear-drops and newness; then quietly, almost secretly, she began to cry as well.

****

From: Joe82@JCIlanguageschool.com
Sent: Mon 26/03/19 8:02 pm
To: girl@hmail.com
Subject: Re: Hey girl!

Girl!

Oh, man. I had the sweetest night last night. We started off at Rio - you remember that bar on

With her one free hand, she hit delete.

****

She was plucked from her dream into a chill, grey, crashing room. 1:17 am. Already. The baby was all around her, the tsunami was all around her and even her sight was at sea.

The cry was surging in peaks and troughs, pulling her nerves, her body with it. She was floating up, gently, and swiftly hurtling down with a smack. Floating, then hurtling. Hurtling, falling. She was falling.

She pulled herself upright again, her eyes open now. She stepped out of the bed to cross the floor. She stood swaying next to the bed, feeling keenly how her breasts and bones ached. Three, four steps towards the cot, she paused and peeked in, and then carried on walking into the bathroom, shutting the bedroom door behind her.

She lay on the floor in a heap and pulled a towel across her back as she sobbed.

****

From: Joe82@JCllanguageschool.com
Sent: Sun 1/04/19 11:23 am
To: girl@hmail.com
Subject: Re: Hey girl!

Hey girl,

It was wonderful to speak to you last night. You sounded a bit withdrawn. Sorry if I was emotional (OK - I admit it - I was tipsy!). It's so hard this long-distance parenting business. I just wish I could be there to experience everything with you.

This semester isn't working out so well and I'm starting to get a bit down. The students just don't seem the same as they were last year: remember Max and Xavier and all that crew? It's been nothing like that buzz this spring. But perhaps that comes from not having you here with me, too.

Jenny sent me a book about fatherhood for my birthday - you must have given her my address? I wondered if it was a dig at first, but the card was lovely with a note about hoping to see me soon, so I am going to take it at face value and say thanks (or at least, hope you'll pass that on for me!). I'll be sure to read it soon.

Take care, both of you,

Joe xxxxxx

****

The cry rose into the night, feline and indecisive. 2.36 a.m. She flicked her eyes open and then blinked hard, to bring things into a clearer focus. She slipped her left foot out of bed onto the coolness and noticed that the floor felt sticky under her feet. A job for the morning.

She had slept without the baby for the first time that afternoon, although it was only in the next room, and only for twenty minutes. A little respite, courtesy of her step-mother. While the baby was being coddled and cuddled and bathed next door, she had sat down in her one and only (but favourite) armchair and closed her eyes. Chuckley sounds and nursery rhymes permeated the air as she drifted off. She had jumped, when she had awoken to Jenny's voice in the room, and found her arms crossed tight across her chest, holding on for dear life to an invisible infant. She shook them out and reached forward to take the baby back.

In the cool night air, she reached the fridge that buzzed in the area of her room that acted as a kitchen - alongside the microwave, kettle, hotplate, two cupboards, a shelf. She opened the fridge door, and grabbed the bottle of formula waiting inside.

****

From: Joe82@JCIlanguageschool.com
Sent: Tues 10/04/19 9:31 pm
To: girl@hmail.com
Subject: Long time no hear...?

Girl,

I've tried calling but your phone is dead, or off. It's been ages since you emailed. All OK?

Love you baby,

Joe x

****

People give you milestones when you have a baby, absolutes: once you get over the birth, your hormones will settle, once your milk comes in, the baby will settle; once you get out of hospital, you'll begin to feel human; once you stop breast-feeding, the baby sleeps longer at night; once you get through the first six weeks, it all falls into place.

It had been six weeks and four days. It was 2.58 a.m.

****

From: Joe82@JCIlanguageschool.com
Sent: Fri 13/04/19 6:40 pm
To: girl@hmail.com
Subject: PLEASE READ

Girl,

Ok - I know why you are ignoring me. I spoke to mum and she says she thinks Lou might have spilled that Joao has offered to extend my contract until the end of the summer. Either way, that cat's out of the bag now, I guess. But you should know that I haven't said yay or nay yet so nothing's definite. That's why I was holding off on telling you. Nothing sinister, honest.

Give me a call so we can talk, yeah?

J xxxx

****

The cry needled persistently into her skin until she was compelled to open her eyes. The baby had gone longer this time - 3.10 a.m. When she padded over into the cot the snuffle was still half-hearted. Looking down, the little, moley eyes twinkled back at her and she thought she saw an attempt at a smile. She smiled back, shocked; shocked, but happy, she swayed and grinned and reached down into the cot to lift the child gently up towards her shoulder.

****

From: Joe82@JCllanguageschool.com
Sent: Tues 17/04/19 4:31 pm
To: girl@hmail.com
Subject:

Girl,

 You're unbelievable. I send you €250 and you still aren't happy. I decide to stay until September - not the end of October as was on offer by the way - so we can have some income and you still blow a gasket. Seriously, have you spoken to the Doctor lately?? I am amazed that you are still talking about going back to Uni. There's plenty of time for that. Yes - I know, I know, we're not 18 anymore but we are still young! At least, I know I am. I thought you wanted to make a go of it, us. You know how I feel about being tied down to one place. At least, I thought you knew how I feel, and I thought I knew how you felt but perhaps I've got it all wrong. The way you were talking on the phone this afternoon I wonder if you want us to be a family at all. THERE IS NO WAY I AM MOVING IN WITH YOUR PIGGING STEP- MOTHER. I can't believe you would even suggest it. I have my pride, you know. Anyway, dad has paid for me to come over to visit for his 60th next Tuesday. I bet that's knocked you for six. It was supposed to be a nice surprise but somehow doesn't seem great timing anymore. If you want to be with me, meet me from the 2:25 plane. I'm sure your blessed 'Jenny- Stepmother-of-the-Year' can help you with the details if you need them. She seems to know everything else these days. I mean it, girl. It's now or never.

 J

****

 The knock on the door made her jump, even though she expected it. 1:31 pm.

She crossed the room in four strides and opened it, and Jenny entered - with a pack of nappies, and a bottle of Champagne.

"These are for you… in a manner of speaking," she said.

"You look fab-u-lous!" she added, breaking the word into three heavy syllables.

There was a pause, as both women glanced down at her purple dress, pretty but a little tight around the tummy. It was the first time she had been out of tracksuit bottoms for weeks.

"So. Don't be nervous. You are doing the right thing. I am sure. We are here for you. We won't let you down. This is the horrible part, the anticipating, and then we can get on with celebrating! You'll be fine; it'll be fine."

A series of staccato sentences streamed from her mouth as Jenny wandered towards the child, happily lying in the baby bouncer, and unclipped the harness.

"Hello there little one…where's my baby? Hey little girl," Jenny murmured.

"Faith. She's called Faith," she corrected, a little too sharply.

"I know love, I know," Jenny spoke slower, quieter. "…So, are you ready?"

"Yes, I think so."

Her step-mother failed to meet her eyes.

"Anyway, you don't have to hurry back you know. I'll take Faith out, and we won't be back until 4.30 at least. If that's OK with you…"

"You know what Jenny, that's fine; do take her out. But I don't know how long I will be out for. Maybe I'll get some sleep?"

Silence, as they looked at each other without blinking. She knew Jenny would want to think she was having fun, moving on, moving up out of the hole she had fallen into. But really, in her own way, she was.

Both women smiled softly. She leant across to smell the scent of her child, her joy, her Faith, and gave her one last kiss on the forehead.

Then she picked up her satchel and headed towards the door - to her University interview, and the day-time, and the outside world.

Sleep on It

His coat was the colour of cinnamon.

The fur had been clipped short, revealing a stocky, squat frame. He had been well fed, they said, and cared for, in his way - but matted and tangled on arrival. The smell was bad. They had shampooed, clipped, preened and now he was a clean and shocked version of his former self. Almost bald, but a few snarled strands remained by his ears; it was as close as they could get without hurting him, they said. He was a flighty little thing and he did not let them handle him.

They called him Hardy; the name the neighbours had said his owner had christened him. They did not say, but it seemed clear Hardy's owner had died – or moved into care, perhaps. A sad tale to match what was clearly, before them, a sad dog.

Of course, we had hoped for a young dog, or a puppy. A dog with no history and bounding with life, a life to roll before him and on into the future, and that we could be a part of. That we could mould. Hardy was at least 10, they said. Aging.

But I knew he was the one. Face weary but watchful, fiercely observant – determined not to miss a trick. And with lambent eyes; irises flickering. They were familiar, and I felt he was mine.

Josh was unsure.

"Listen Jayne," he said, as we sat drinking coffee after our first visit, "I get it. You want to save him. And yeah... well... he was gorgeous. He was. But it's not what we said, is it babe? What we agreed?"

Josh looked through the steam of his mug at me. Drank a large swig to indicate he had said his piece. His eyes always looked a little damp, gleaming, somehow. Always a little humid. And yet his face was strong, belied this.

"I know, I know," I replied, "I know we did. But we can help him, Josh. And that was before we went there. They don't have any young dogs, anyway, do they? And they said it could be ages. They never get them!"

He raised one eyebrow at me. Continued to drink his coffee.

"Hardly ever get them," I corrected.

He sighed.

"Let's sleep on it: talk about it again tomorrow."

He did this often. If he didn't enjoy the way the conversation was going, he simply stopped it. It was a gift he had, and he could pass it off as reason, logic. Initially, I hadn't even noticed, but as the first few months had dissolved behind us and we became established as a proper, solid couple, I had started to notice that we were sleeping on things more and more. And now that we had been together almost two years, I had started to anticipate it – and so often I was the Princess, with the little pea of a plea, an idea, or an issue we needed to resolve poking through the mattress at me, keeping me awake and worried, wondering all night.

Josh did not like confrontation, arguments, shouting. The slightest hint of passion and he was gone – emotionally, and often physically. He did not engage. He did not speak. He was a solid block, a concrete block and it was infuriating. I wanted to shake him, to make the cracks appear. But he was steadfast. Bombproof. He did not fracture. Did not show any gaps. He was set.

His saving grace was that he did reflect. During his time away, his time of silence, he processed things and then when he came back; sometimes he would agree with me, or apologise. I could live with this.

Though the waiting, in between, was painful.

The next morning, he announced that we should ask to take him for a walk. Not a full victory but a step towards one. Relief tingled on my skin, but I tried to hide my excitement. We had already been vetted by the shelter, who had visited our home, asked us questions - and when

I called them, and they said we could take him the next day, a Saturday, for a two-hour trial.

It was the Friday evening before the trial, and we were going for dinner. It was our anniversary. We did not go crazy with these things – I suspected it would unsettle Josh if we did – but we did always acknowledge them, happily, comfortably.

He was an affectionate man, in spite of it all.

I had chosen the restaurant, a little fragrant Italian that we had been to several times before.

"You don't mind, do you? I know it's not exciting," I asked him, as we danced around each other while dressing.

"No, sweetheart, I know you love it there," he paused and gave a little kiss on my forehead. "I like it too," he added.

The restaurant was busy and dark, yet the atmosphere was vibrant. The tables were close together and an ant-farm of waiters skilfully manoeuvred the room in patterns, dropping bread baskets on tables, topping up wine glasses. It was heady, scented, warm. It was perfect.

After our starters, Josh asked the waiter if we could have a short break between courses. I was surprised, he hadn't asked me if I minded, and this seemed out of character. It was one of his traits, his 'are you sure?'s.

"Why did you do that?" I asked, half-joking, as the waiter stepped away. "Some of us want our risotto."

Josh looked at me seriously, with his dark, glossy eyes. He frowned, just a little, and tipped his head forward, leant in until his hair, usually brushed back so neatly, flopped down onto his face.

"What's the matter?"

It was the dog, I thought. He'd changed his mind about the dog.

"Will you marry me?" he said.

I lifted my left hand to my face, placed the middle three fingers against my lips. Shocked. He stared at me, eyes pleading, glistening.

I dropped my hand to the table.

"Yes," I said.

The next day, we drove into town to look in jewellery shops before we were due at the shelter. Josh – rarely one to show more than brooding, suppressed emotion – was excitable. Almost giddy.

"I think I know what you'd like," he said, "I know you don't like bling, but I didn't want to get it wrong. It's your ring: you should get to choose it."

In the old town was a street with five or six jewellers, a mix of very old, established family shops and modern chains. In the second shop we went in, we found several we both loved. I wanted to buy one then and there – found a traditional ring with one small, rectangular diamond in the centre and a clutch of others around it. Not too big, not too flashy. But beautiful.

I was my usual self – decisive, quick, impulsive.

"Shall we get it now?" I asked, excitedly. I could see his unease. He was not one for being rushed.

"I think we should put it aside," he said, "Sleep on it."

We collected Hardy from the shelter, along with a long list of instructions, and a little bag of his things. He seemed excited to be going out with us, but at the same time weary. His feet itched forward and then back a little in a shuffle as he twitched to go out the door, but he stared up at us, ears and eyes alert for trouble.

We took him to the beach, a twenty-minute drive away.

"Are you happy?" Josh asked me in the car, knowing I was, but wanting to hear it again, I guessed.

"Ecstatic," I said, and rubbed his arm gently.

"I suppose we need to think about wedding dates and things now," he pretended to drop his head to the steering wheel in despair, glanced over to me with a smile.

"Will you invite your mum?" I asked, quickly.

"No."

He looked at the road, firmly.

"Oh, but will you tell her? Will you tell her you are getting married?"

"No, Jayne. Why would I? I haven't spoken to her in three years. She doesn't even know you exist. What would it mean to her?"

"But you could just send her a message or something, it might be a good opportunity to…"

He reached over and squeezed my right knee.

"I don't want to," he said in a small but sure voice.

The wall was there again, and the stale smell of his history hung faintly in the air. A recognisable scent but one I could not place, with so many gaps in my knowledge, such little information to go on. I could not understand it – how could I? And yet I loved this man, with his quirks, and his mysteries. I did not want to push him, to make him sad. He was so often just a little sad.

At the beach, Hardy came alive. The years fell away from him as he bounded along the hard, compact sand. It was damp and firm, almost concrete but with a little give, and a filigree surface.

On his long lead, he would charge ahead of us, then sit and watch as we caught up, sitting still and facing the wind. The air was damp, and I was unsure if this was from drizzle, mist or the spray of the top tufts of the high tide nearby, onto the breeze.

He ran with his ball in his mouth; dropped it; ran after it again as Josh threw it.

"He's a well-trained dog," Josh said. I linked arms with him, and walked along, marvelling at the air and the ease and the warmth among the three of us.

From nowhere, a large dog – a lurcher, maybe? – came running up. Hardy raced back to our side, a new dog, a different dog. His gently wagging tail was replaced by a stiff, erect one. His ears pricked, his chest forward. He began to bark, a timbre to the sound we had not heard before. The two dogs leapt at each other, not quite in attack, but almost so, and Hardy placed his front paws around the collar of the other, even though he was the larger animal - cuffing the top of his head and back of his neck.

Stunned, and inexperienced as we were, we did not know what to do. Josh began to raise his voice with ineffectual commands, and I tried to shorten the lead, pull Hardy to me, but he was yanking the tangled mess into knots and bows around all of our legs.

The noise was thunderous, proud.

The dog's owner came jogging up, an ageing man, apologetic, out of breath.

"I don't know what happened," he said, "He's never done that before."

"Don't worry, they were both at fault," Josh replied, as the man clipped a lead on his dog, confidently, and the pair were pulled away from each other.

But it was clear to me that Hardy was the protagonist.

Shaken, we started to make our way back to the car, on a shorter lead. Hardy seemed completely to have forgotten the incident, and walked a little ahead, tail and ears up, with a slight pant and a spring in his step.

We didn't speak, walked swiftly until we got back to the carpark.

"I guess he's a work in progress," Josh said, quietly, as he opened the boot.

I let him place Hardy in the car, watching as the dog allowed Josh to assist his back legs that didn't quite reach the space, where he had tried to jump up, ineffectually, unpractised. Watching this gentle man and this damaged dog, the pair of them brave and docile and cautious. The pair of them guarded, unsure. Josh leant into the boot, ruffling the bristles of fur on his back. Hardy settled down, curled his front paws around a little, almost under himself.

Josh shut the boot and stayed still, leaving his hand on the latch.

"It won't be easy," he stated. And then, "Do you want to sleep on it?"

So, it was up to me then. I felt a little shift beneath my feet, a change.

"No," I said, "I don't think I do. Sometimes it's worth the effort."

We looked at each other, his eyes bright, burnished. I felt the fear, the gratitude, the love, and the future ahead – ours to mould – wrap around us.

Incendiary

Saturday – 12:35 am

    It was the noise that hit me first. A wail, a guttural yowl, that sliced the air. I thought it was something artificial, amplified. But, no - this was real. Human.
    At the window, I could see light humming through the curtains, aglow. I jumped from my bed, head behind the rest of me: still attached to the pillow; still moulded to my sleep. My hair was a web across my neck, sticky with sweat and dreams. My t-shirt, a knot that swirled behind my back and constricted my arms, my movement. I shook myself out – pulled myself together.
    I drew the curtains back and saw it: the fire, the flames, the destruction. Glints of sparks flew from the downstairs window – or the place where it should have been – shooting with force and light, like bullets. Dark smoke rolled from the top of the gap, out into the night air. Murky, almost black, flotsam and jetsam. I opened my window and the thick air clogged my airways.
    Her house was destroyed.
    And there - as a dog, a wolf, a banshee - she crouched on the floor in the street, knees scraping the tarmac, scrambling, rising to her feet, then falling. Rising, then falling. Screaming.
    Like a slaughtered pig.

    ****

Friday – 7:20 pm

    Around at Amy's house, I arrived with a bottle of wine and my mobile. She was going out and I was babysitting her daughter, and her mum, Liz, in a way.
    Liz was nodding on the sofa as I entered the house, already fighting bedtime. Her head was dropping and then jerking upright. She was worn down, smaller, thinner each time I saw her; hollow-boned. A little bird.

Amy was effervescent, visibly excited to be going out for once. She chattered as she moved around the house, tucking things in, putting things away. It made me blush. Her place was always spotless – in sharp relief to mine. She even had fresh cut flowers on the table, for God's sake. Amy was clean sheets, crisply ironed shirts, open windows, hand-washed dishes. She was immaculate: remarkable in this way.

She shuffled Liz upstairs, propped her in bed with a remote control for a portable television and a glass of orange cordial by her bedside.

Then she was ready.

"I won't be late," she said, grinning.

"Be as late as you like," I replied, "You don't get out often," I paused. "No offence."

She laughed.

"See you at 10:30."

The moment the front door was closed the tears overwhelmed me. I sagged down onto the sofa, the relief at not having to remain calm, act as expected, was immense. I had spent the day in pretence of normality but now I was overcome. This was not normal.

I was still holding the bottle of wine in my hand and so I placed it between my two knock-knees as I bent over, doubled up, sobbing. I unscrewed the top, one-handed, and then swigged straight from the bottle with a huge, satisfying glug, gratifyingly messily. I wiped one sleeve across my face to remove the splattered alcohol and tears.

Then I took the note from my pocket: Steve's handwriting, and yet it wasn't written for me. 'Love you,' it said, 'Can't wait to see you again soon. Call me when…' but it was cut off. I kept looking back to it, away and back, hoping to see that sentence completed. When did he want calling? Who did he want to call him? How could he do this? And why was he writing notes – why not calling, texting?

Then it struck me why: because I paid the bills.

So, I was sitting at home figuring out our household accounts and he was off leaving notes for another woman.

It had been folded up in his shirt pocket. I went to put it in the wash but a faint smell of perfume, a puff of the feminine, had caught my attention as I grabbed it from the washing basket to shove it into the machine. It had brought me back into the room, snapped me from routine, and so I had stopped what I was doing and had stared at that shirt, held up high by my right hand, fist balled around the collar. I had a feeling. A tingle. I stopped, sniffed, and then noted the lump in the top pocket.

And that's when I had found it.

Here I was now, a good six hours later, sat on my neighbour's sofa, drinking wine from a bottle and wondering what to do next. Luckily, I hadn't had to see him. He was going straight out for a 'work do' – or so he said – and had texted me to say he would be home by 11.

'C ya l8r,' he had written.

It took me a while to even unpick the sense of it. Text speak. Like a teenager. How much time had he gained, by curtailing it like that? Was I not even worth an extra ninety seconds?

So, I had become a 'C ya'. And this other woman – whoever she was – had become his, 'Love you'.

I stayed, sat, bottle wedged between limbs, periodically sniffing and swigging, until the room turned dark and I noticed I was cold, hungry. I stood up, and realised I was unsteady. Realised I had already drunk most of the wine, in a little under an hour, and that I was feeling leaden, cloudy from it.

Undulating as I stepped, I wandered into the kitchen and made myself toast, greedily - the bread hardly brown, my impatience popping the toaster up after less than a minute. I had not eaten since breakfast. Lukewarm bread and wine from a bottle, it was then. And, where was he? No doubt quaffing expensive whisky and wolfing down some finnicky, tasteful meal in a high-end restaurant. Paying by cash, leaving no trail. Leaning in, leaning close to her hair and scent and the taste of her, to nibble her neck and ear and invite her off somewhere to…

I dropped the butter-knife with a crack onto the tiled floor, unsure if I had done this intentionally, and yet curiously tempted to do it again. The sound had been satisfying. But no, I could not, as I might wake Liz, or little Sophie.

Then the thought of that shirt popped into my mind again. I had dropped that too, allowed it to fold itself into a defeated heap on top of the rest of the washing - and I had not returned to it. And now that scented shirt, with its filth and guilt and secrets, was contaminating the laundry. Infecting everything.

I needed to wash it clean.

****

Friday – 8:50 pm

I ran across the street, barefoot - panting before I had even started. I was in my head as I ran, my feet a long way from me, unfeeling, my senses heightened around my face, my ears – air sharp, skin cold on my cheeks - and ears burning, almost hurting as I went. I could hear my own breath, gasping loudly, and my voice around me, unsure if it was in my head or spoken aloud.

"Get the shirt."

I went down the side of the house and through the backdoor. I had left it unlocked, as I was wont to do, and it opened into a small lobby. Scruffy, I noted, shocked and suddenly present, to see the contrast with Amy's home. Black scuff-marks from discarded boots scarred the walls; the carpet was dirty, almost threadbare at the entrance.

Straight ahead of me was the door to the back of the garage. I opened it and saw again the mound of tangled cotton with that shirt – the evidence - strewn on top.

My stomach lurched, and a small heap of red wine vomit heaved to the back of my throat. I swallowed it down, moved forward to do what I had to do. I grabbed the shirt by one cuff and jogged back to Amy's, trailing it behind me, on the damp tarmac - my white flag.

****

Friday – 9:10 pm

Amy had a proper utility room boxed off at the back of her garage. It had been boarded and plastered and painted a fresh yellow. She had deep, pine shelves with a range of plastic washing baskets sitting, as train carriages, along them. Clothes, sorted by colour, were piled in some. The whites were quite full, but the black basket had just a few items in it. Some hampers were empty. She even had a green basket – a green basket! – where a neat hillock of jades and ferns and olives sat, waiting to be washed.

I opened the washing machine, which was empty, of course, and threw the shirt inside with two pods of detergent. I turned the dial to 'hot' and set the machine into action - then I opened the fridge, which was sat next to the machine, and reached for the bottle of white wine that I knew would be in there.

****

Friday – 10:30 pm

The white wine was over half gone. I had upgraded to a glass and sat at the dining table, my consumption slowed slightly by the crafting of a document – a letter of sorts – on my phone. I had to keep re-reading and correcting, my fingers and thoughts clumsy with alcohol and emotion. I was writing it out as a note, collected enough to know that it was dangerous to write it in an email, that at any time I might hit 'send' in a fit of hubris, or anger.

The words were barbed and charged, and they clanged together on the screen: bastard; vain; ridiculous; hypocrite.

Fucker.

A timer bleeped on my phone, reminding me of the shirt, that would be sitting in the machine, now clean but damp.

I staggered to the utility room, turning on lights as I went, and suddenly noticing a cut on my left foot. It must have been there since I went outside, but I hadn't noted it before. A few little drops of my blood had trailed on the floor earlier, it seemed, and now dried dark and dotted like a mud splatter. I made it to the washing machine and pulled out the damp shirt – its scent now neutral, doused in the familiar smell of domesticity.

Above the washing machine, a tumble drier was on a thick shelf. I chucked the shirt in, then realised the machine had no power. I hammered on buttons, inelegant fingers jabbing, missing, having no impact. Then I found the plug socket, cursed my foolishness, and flipped the switch. The display came to life and several buttons were flashing. I ignored them, turned the dial around as far as it would go, and hoped for the best. It started to drone.

I wandered back into the house, pushing doors wide with the flat of my hand, turning off lights behind me. I caught the sound of someone padding about upstairs and froze temporarily – worried Sophie might appear and how I would cope with this. But the noise soon stopped. I seemed to be in the clear: it must have been Liz.

Then I found my shoes and sat on the sofa, slipped them on, to put away my dirty feet, the blood, their reminders.

****

Friday – 10:55 pm

Amy burst through the living room door and flicked the light on.

"Oh!" she cried, "Sorry!"

I jumped, confused for a moment - unsure where I was and who this person was before me. I was jolted back into the space. I had fallen asleep.

Amy was rosy, tipsy, happy. She seemed oblivious to my desolate and drunk state. So, I did not speak, hoped she would attribute this to doziness.

She walked straight in and started taking off her jewellery, taking down her hair.

"Did anyone wake?"

"Liz did," I slurred, "But all OK"

"Oh?" she turned to me, one hand to her ear, fiddling with an earring.

I just shrugged, pushed myself upright, and fumbled for my phone.

"Knackered, sorry," I said.

I could hear myself, thinking I sounded odd, far away, and that surely, she would notice. But she didn't appear to – she was locked inside some little cloud of bliss and I did not permeate.

She was smiling gently to herself while she started to unclip her necklace. I moved towards the door.

"Bye!" she called, "Thanks!"

I let myself out.

****

Saturday – 12:41 am

I don't know why I was so shocked by the heat. It was a forcefield, stopping me from moving closer than the front gate. I tried, I lunged in, but the smoke filled my nostrils and the smell and temperature seemed to singe my nasal hair, eyelashes.

Around me, sounds, scents, a fire engine, a police car. An audience.

Steve appeared, threw one arm across me.

"Back!" he yelled.

I turned to look for Amy again. She was curled into a ball, rocking, wailing, rubbing her cheek across the tarmac and periodically lifting her head towards the house and calling. I couldn't understand her words. But I knew. I knew. Someone was still in there.

At last, through the front door came a fire-fighter, and cradled in his arms was a shape, a form, wrapped in a towel or sheet, misshapen. And not moving.

****

Saturday – 6:17 pm

We were sat in Liz's house, two streets from home. A living room full of neighbours and well-wishers. I hadn't been in here for over two years, and it was a strange mix of comfortably familiar with washed out, dull, grimy, sepia: it was untouched since Liz had come to stay with Amy, around eighteen months ago.

Steve was with me. He sat perched, on the arm of the sofa, looking dirty and defeated. I was glad he was there, though we had hardly spoken since we had awoken in the small hours. I almost couldn't remember what I knew to be truth, what he knew of it. Everything was tumbled in my mind, tangled.

Amy sat in the midst of it all, in a borrowed dressing gown, with damp hair, and cradling a hot toddy in a mug.

Jill was talking, telling us all what she knew, quietly, yet publicly, as if Amy wasn't even there, or couldn't hear, somehow.

"They said it started in the garage or the utility room. They aren't allowed to say, officially like, until they have finished their – you know – investigations. Just in case. In case, you know. But anyway, it is pretty obvious it started in the garage. It's completed burnt out there. And then it spread to the downstairs. Trapped them."

"But I don't get it. Why would it start in the garage?"

It was an older lady I didn't recognise, who spoke. She stared intently at Jill, as if she must have all the answers; looking for some certainty amongst the chaos.

"Something electrical. The garage, or utility. She had a fridge in there. A dryer."

And as she said the word the ground fell below me, all around me, until I was still, exposed, vulnerable, unsteady on a pinnacle. On a ladder. Gallows.

"Oh, I see," the woman said. "The fridge."

"Or the dryer," Jill repeated.

"I don't think speculating is helpful," I said, too loudly, in a voice that was high, tight.

I tiptoed off my summit, staggered across to the sofa, where Amy was sat. The fire had consumed its own evidence. Who knew if they would ever determine what happened? And yet I did, I knew. Doors open. Machine on. Lights flashing. Dial too far. One shirt; only one shirt for all the heat. One dirty, filthy shirt. Lint. Pine. Electricity. Lies.

I squeezed myself between her and her brother, Will, who was staring into his own hands, unspeaking. I could feel Amy shivering, beside me. Her brother warm, smelling of coffee.

"Do you want me to call Dave?" I asked, quietly.

Dave was Sophie's dad. She shook her head.

"I did it," she said.

That afternoon, I had been in to see Liz at the hospital. The image of her was seared into me, lying in bed, her translucent skin crinkled across a thin frame and in sharp relief against the white sheets. She was wearing a patterned and frayed hospital gown, with short sleeves. Her purple veins were a vine across her skin, and bloomed into a large bruise on her upper arm where she had been grabbed, perhaps, or fallen. She did not open her eyes.

I was not allowed to see Sophie.

Amy had been there all day. She had some smoke inhalation, and a few cuts and bruises, but nothing serious – and she had been ricocheting from one ward to another.

I had not seen her cry. She seemed strangely composed, together, and she asked insightful questions of the Doctors and nurses. But they had asked her repeatedly to go home, to look after herself, to shower, to rest. There was nothing she could do here, they said. And she needed to save her own strength.

Eventually, her sister arrived, having driven for five or six hours, and after a short while Amy relinquished her post, and went home to bathe.

She planned to go back soon; she had made this clear to all of us.

"Where are you staying tonight, love?" asked the strange woman.

Amy shrugged.

"Here?" I ventured.

"Probably."

"You can't stay here alone," said her brother. "I have to get back for the kids. Or I could ring someone, try to sort it?"

"Don't know," was all she said.

"Will's right, love," said the woman again, "you shouldn't stay here alone."

"I'll stay," Steve spoke, suddenly, "I don't mind."

Amy looked at him. And I saw it. I saw what passed between them. And I thought I would fall again. I thought I would fall down onto the ground and I would scream, like a banshee, like a slaughtered pig, because I knew. Just then, I knew: something was in there, inside that brief look, something that could not be undone.

The phone started to ring, and the room froze, and so I was captured; I was a moth in amber, stuck in that moment in time. In the terror.

Jill answered it: we heard her murmur from the hallway, and then the pad of her feet across Liz's tiled floor. Everyone listened, watched.

She came back into the room, eyes wet, glinting, wide.

"Amy," she said, her voice unsteady, "It's the hospital."

And Amy crumpled in on herself, a concertina, a crumbling paper fan, while Steve – my husband, my soulmate, my love – threw his arms around her shoulders, and wept.

French Knitting on a Cotton Reel

I don't know why I took the ring.

I went into the bathroom, and when I went to wash my hands, noticed the gold hoop sitting by the side of the sink. It was sparkling, beguiling - a miniature halo.

My hands were soapy and warm as I tried to put the engagement ring on; it wouldn't push past my knuckle, gnarled and ugly as it was. So, I tried my little finger, and it slipped on: the cold metal rolling with ease around the base. The clear, white stone – a diamond, presumably – winked as it twisted. I pulled it off and dropped it into my cardigan pocket, then I grabbed some tissue and balled it into a cloud to shove on top of it and keep it safe. True.

Back in the lounge and the party had finished, so only a handful of people were milling about, tidying up. The room was dim and musty. Ian sat on the couch, swigging from a tin can, while around him Martha was dropping glass into a green bag, one heavy item at a time, rhythmically. Slowly. Leaning near him and over him to grab an empty water bottle, a Prosecco bottle. He didn't flinch.

Across the room, from the dining table, in synchronicity, Jeff was scooping paper plates and crisp packets into a white bag.

Ian sat still, comfortable in the nucleus of the action. Slowly raising one arm, periodically, to take a leisurely swig. He stared ahead.

Ellie reappeared, her purple dress now replaced with pyjamas and her hair pulled back. She was tired, and more than a little tipsy. She was gently smiling.

Martha paused and looked at her, with some surprise.

"I thought you'd gone to bed," she said.

"I feel bad leaving you lot to clean up; you don't even live here!"

Ian does, I thought. But I said nothing.

"Love, you've had a long day. Get some rest," Martha said.

"It's only 10 pm," Ellie replied, "I can lie in tomorrow, mum."

"Go to bed, Ellie," Ian said, firmly. Everyone looked at him. He lifted his head, and gave one of his little smiles. "Sweetheart, you should go to bed."

"OK then," she said, a little confused, "Night mum."

She went over and gave Martha a kiss.

"I'll pop around tomorrow," I called over as she approached the stairs.

"Thanks, Nan," she replied.

****

The next day, I spent the morning running little errands. I pushed all thoughts of engagement rings, and theft, to the back of my mind, balled and cocooned inside the tissue and hidden away. Every now and then it would begin to unfurl, threaten to roll out into my consciousness. But I would not allow this. I couldn't bear to think on what I had done.

Lunchtime, and a text from Ellie told me she was now up and functioning, if I wanted to pop around. I went to one more shop and then drove the short distance to her house, bringing with me a little box of cakes.

She answered the door in a tracksuit, with wet hair and a clean face.

"Nan!" she cried, happy to see me, "Come in!"

"Cakes," I said, as I thrust the white box forward into her hands.

"Ooo," she said as she took them, "But I ate my weight in saturated fat last night as it is."

The house was clean and tidy again, and Ian nowhere to be seen. The windows were ajar, back door agape, the space light, bright, open.

"Where's Ian?" I asked.

"Oh, he decided to meet up with Gary for lunch, because he couldn't make it to the party. You know, Gary? They've gone to the pub. I don't expect I'll see him for hours!"

The little ball of paper started to unfold again in my mind, like a frond, a fern leaf. I snapped it closed.

Ellie brought plates in from the kitchen and I could hear the kettle starting to boil.

"Tea?" she asked.

She was placing mats on the table and I looked down to see her left hand, no ring, red nail varnish slightly chipped on her index finger. She looked down too. Her hand stopped moving. There was a beat.

"I can't find my ring, Nan,"

I thought she would cry.

"Since when?" I said.

I didn't know what else to say, do. I didn't know how I should react. My thoughts were unballing. But I could not confess.

"I'm not sure," she said, unsteadily, "But I haven't seen it at all today."

"Do you usually take it off? Did you take it off when you went to bed, perhaps? I'm sure we'll find it. You haven't been anywhere, so it must be in the house."

"I know, I've been telling myself that. But I have searched everywhere and there's no sign. I'm worried it's in with the rubbish or something."

"I'm sure it's not, love. I'm certain," and I went over to her and gently rubbed her forearm, was surprised by how cool her skin felt against my warm, rough hands. She lifted her right hand to her face.

"Ian told me I drank too much last night. I thought he was overreacting – I mean, it was a party after all, but then… this. Maybe he was right. Oh, God."

We stood still in the chill and the bright and I continued to rub her arm, slowly.

"I am sure you will find it," I said, "But you know, love, even if you don't, it's not the end of the world. Nothing is irreplaceable."

She went back into the kitchen and I could hear cupboards, crockery, domestic sounds. By the time she came back to the dining table she seemed more herself. She passed me a mug of tea and nudged a plate bearing an éclair, indicating I should take it. We sat in comfortable silence for a little while.

"When met your grandad," I said, "neither of us had any money. People didn't really do engagements in those days, not like they do now, with parties and long waits before the wedding. But he wanted to give me a ring. Was desperate. Wanted to give me something.

He came around one evening to take me out, to dance, and as we walked along the road he started to tell me about how his little sister had been finger knitting – do you know finger knitting? And she'd been spool knitting using a cotton reel to hold the threads, making little knitted strands and then sewing them together to make egg cosies. French knitting, we used to call it."

I took a bite of my cake, a swig of tea. Ellie sat still and stared at the plate, dabbing a finger in the crumbs.

"Well," I continued, "He was going on about this finger knitting and French knitting and I wondered what he was so excited about. Bouncing he was, walking just a bit ahead of me and looking back, walking backwards in parts. I can still see it now.

And then he told me his little sister had shown him how to do it. She had taught him how to wind the little threads around the pins in the spool, and make the pattern of knots to create a tube of knitting.

'I made this,' he says to me, and produces something from his pocket. Stops walking.

I thought it would be an egg cosy. Felt sure this was why he was so animated. He had made me an egg cosy. Bless him.

But no, when I looked down there was a little knitted ring in his hand. A little, brownish knitted ring. He had made it for me. He had unpicked his woollen scarf, taken the threads, and made me a ring. Can you believe that?"

I had been transported by my own story; had almost forgotten where I was. For a moment I had felt again the rush of tingles that had enveloped me from my feet to my head in that moment; I smelt the damp air after summer rain; I was wrapped in the heady pressure, the intensity of our love.

Then I was back in the room; I felt his loss again, briefly, acutely.

I looked up at Ellie, staring at me, amazed, with tears in her eyes.

****

Three days later, and I had a call from Ellie inviting me around to collect some tomatoes. She had heaps of them, she said, from the garden. And Ian was sick of them.

She did not mention the ring.

I decided to walk the short distance to her home, as I hadn't been out all day; early evening and the sky was still light, the air fresh but pleasant. I wore thin woollen gloves to protect my arthritic fingers, just the same. In the right pocket of my jacket I had slipped the ring, wrapped in a fresh tissue. As I swung my arms, I periodically felt the lump of it, rhythmically and repeatedly brushing against my forearm and reminding me what I had done. What I had done. What I had done.

Earlier that day, I had taken her ring and placed it on my little finger, marvelling at its beauty against my craggy, sallow skin.

It was time.

When I arrived at the house it was almost 6. Ellie was not long home from work: hair pulled into a bun, little pinch of a frown between her eyebrows.

"Come in, Nan," she said and walked away from the door before I had even entered.

"I can come back?" I called after her.

"What?" she turned slightly, "No, sorry. I've just had a hard day."

I shut the door behind me and walked straight towards the kitchen to get her a cup of tea. I slipped off my right glove and set about making it.

"Work?"

"Yes, work… and then I just called Ian from the bus. We had a bit of a… a sort of row. Sort of."

"Oh," was all I said.

She started a gentle ricochet from one piece of furniture to another, picking up a motoring magazine, moving a pair of men's shoes, a man's watch, a dirty pint glass: collecting random things and settling them in their rightful places, or at the foot of the stairs, ready to go away.

"He finished work early, but he says he's in the pub," she said, and then, more quietly, "again."

I put a teapot on the table and placed down two coasters, two mugs, a pint of milk.

"Sit down, love," I said.

"I was thinking about your story, Nan. Your ring story."

I looked at her, but she didn't meet my gaze.

"He did that for you. Grandad did that for you," she gave a gentle shake of her head. A look of wonder on her face.

"I chose my own ring, you know," she continued, "He hadn't bought one when he proposed. He even suggested I go to pick it out without him, he offered to give me his credit card - but I made him come, I forced him. And then, when he was there, he wanted to get some ludicrously expensive ring, even bigger than the one we settled on. I was excited at the time. I thought it was proof that he did care about it after all. But you know what? That ring's been missing for four days, and he hasn't even noticed. He hasn't even noticed."

"You haven't found it then," was all I could think to say. She shook her head.

"I think I'd feel weird, wearing it now, to be honest. That one week when I was wearing it. I was ecstatic. But now it's gone, and everything is normal again. And I don't feel ecstatic. I don't. But I should. Even without the ring, I should. Right?"

We had rarely spoken like this. Rarely been so frank. But I could see the desperation in her. The need. She was raw and vulnerable, the underbelly of a cat: looking for comfort, exposed. Looking to be soothed.

But I could not do it.

"I'm sure you'll find the ring," I said. She winced, shook her head, just a little, was about to speak, "But –" I interjected, quickly, "That doesn't mean you have to wear it."

She looked up.

"It's an engagement ring," I said. "Not a wedding ring."

Then, I slipped my right hand into the jacket pocket. I pulled out the bundle of tissue and dropped it on the table. Ellie watched as I unpeeled the hankie with my two-coloured hands. My right hand contorted and pale, with a little tremor, as it shed layers of white paper away, slowly. My left hand still gloved, the wool smoothing over the cracks and bumps, disguising the passage of time.

We both looked down at the prize.

The little, woollen ring lay in the mounds of paper, frayed and fuzzed by time.

Ellie was entranced, she reached over to pick it up, urgently, but then hesitated just as her fingers brushed the threads.

"Can I?" she asked.

I nodded, and she picked the ring up between forefinger and thumb, with keen and precise dexterity - as if picking a flower, a daisy. A four-leafed clover.

"I'm sorry," I said.

She looked at me, confused - and then watched again – still with the ring poised high, as I peeled the glove from my left hand to reveal her engagement ring on my little finger.

She said nothing.

For a long while, we sat still and quiet. She rolled the woollen ring in the light, as if trying to conjure a sparkle that was not there. On the table between us the diamonds lay still, flat and inconsequential. I sipped my tea.

Then the front door slammed. There was immediate noise, and smells, and a change in the air around us as a draught blew through while he entered the house. He was whistling, brushing into things, and I could hear him throwing a coat on the sofa, shoes on the floor. Calling out.

"Ellie?"

"In here," she said, distracted still, by the ring between her fingers.

He came in and stood about a metre away from us – arms slightly out to the side, legs slightly apart. Steadying himself. I gazed at him, but she did not acknowledge him.

"What's going on?"

She placed the woollen ring down on the table, next to the diamond one: the two loops forming an asymmetrical pair, just touching. The hard, bright freshness of the newer one leant against the warm, worn softness of the other.

"I need to talk to you," she said.

Acknowledgements

Thank you to Sara-Jane, for proofreading and encouragement. Thank you to Stuart, Carol, Mandy and Julia for beta-reading feedback.

And thank you to you, lovely Mx. Reader, for buying my book, and reading this far. You've always been my favourite one.